I0603812

JUNE FOSTER

A Home in Cranberry Cove

June Foster

He says, "Be still and know that I am God; I will be exalted among the nations, I will be exalted in the earth." Psalm 46:10 (NIV)

Chapter One

Madison Mitchell climbed the wooden stairs to Sloan's Fishing Supplies. Why not check out the store where her long, lost boyfriend used to work? Ha, who was she kidding? Ryder Langston had never been hers.

She passed the military museum and paused at the next window—an exclusive gift shop where the least expensive item would cost too much for her budget. Her budget strained by her recent circumstances—single and living on a teacher's salary.

A stained-glass piece hanging in the window caught her eye. The picture depicted a summer woodland scene with rock stairs leading into a forest of Douglas fir and then fading into the distance.

She took a few steps closer as a tingle tickled her skin. Where did the stairs lead? Perhaps to a life better than the one she led now. A life where a husband valued her instead of divorcing her and leaving for another woman. Somehow, she knew the answer was important.

She meandered on to the last store. Since the first day Ryder had hired the assistant manager, the window displays had become more appealing, more professionally designed than some she'd seen in Seattle.

In the window, a display with a mannequin dressed in green chest waders stood next to fishing nets, colorful lures, and a variety of reels. The model raised a fly rod over his head, ready to cast. A ferocious bear on two hind legs hovered over the man as if ready to attack. Replicas of miniature, stately firs shaded a sparkling, blue pond.

The bell dinged as Madison walked through the door.

"Be right with you," a person called from the back.

She strolled toward the display. The fly rod in the model's hand didn't look much different than the rod her father used the times he took her fishing when she was a child.

A rack of fly rods sat next to the window. She reached for one, lifted out the pole, and took several steps back into the aisle. Yep, she'd used one of these before, and she had plenty of room. With a flick of her wrist, she waved the rod backward over her head as her father had taught her. The handle slipped out of her grip and flew through the air behind her.

Whack.

"Ow."

"Oh, no." Madison whirled around.

A man held his head and grimaced.

She pressed her hands on either side of her cheeks. "Oh, dear."

The guy swept his dark hair off his forehead and rubbed a red spot on his jaw. "The end of your fly rod caught me on the side of my face."

Madison glanced at the rod lying on the floor and

then up to the man again. "I'm so sorry." She took a few steps toward him to examine his cheek. "I, er, I don't know what got into me." How could she tell him she'd relived her childhood memory of going fishing with her father?

The man's nametag read *Micah Collins, General Manager*. His dark eyes twinkled with mischief as he reached down to pick up the rod. "Will this be cash or card?"

She drew her hand to her chest. "I hadn't planned on purchasing the rod. Was it damaged?"

"Nope. But I figured you might want to get out on the stream and practice casting."

"I suppose you're right." But going fishing was the last thing on her mind right now.

"With a purchase, we have individual and group fishing lessons available if you're interested. I'd suggest you take a couple."

Warmth heated Madison's cheek. Now this guy was teasing her. Or maybe he wanted to make light of the awkward situation. "Yes, I'm sure you're right. But I don't get much time off."

"No, problem. We teach at your convenience." The store manager replaced the rod on the rack. "Are you interested in stream or ocean fishing?"

"I think stream would suit me better. Who are the instructors?"

Micah smiled. "I'm one. But I think I'll assign another of our fishing guides to you." He laughed. "Not sure I can survive any more wallops from your rod."

"I'll definitely not do that again." Madison glanced around the well-stocked store. "So, you took Ryder Langston's place when he left?"

"Yes. I was assistant manager for nine months until Ryder married." Micah handed her a rod. "Try this one out for size. Did you know Ryder?"

"Yes." No need to explain more. Madison turned toward the counter. The least she could do would be to buy a rod and sign up. "This one seems good to me. I think I better get my name on the list for fishing lessons."

Micah chuckled. "You think?" He pulled a clipboard from the checkout desk. "Here we go. Give me your name, phone number, and the type of fishing you'd like to do. We'll get back to you and arrange a convenient time." He rang up her purchase. "Unless you plan to use it before the lesson, I can keep it here and bring it with me on the day of the lesson."

Madison filled out the information and returned the form to Micah. "I'd appreciate it if you could hold on to it."

Micah glanced at the notebook. "Madison Mitchell. I've lived here almost a year and haven't met you."

She swallowed hard. No way she'd tell him six months ago she was trying to teach school and make her marriage work. She restrained the sigh that begged to escape her lips.

"Besides shopping in fishing supply stores, what do you do?"

She twirled a strand of hair around her finger. "I'm a teacher at the high school, but I'm off for the summer."

"Must be nice to have the time off to travel."

Travel? No such luck. "Actually, I'm working at the inn this summer helping my best friend, Ashton Atwood." And trying to forget about how things turned out with Josh.

The uncomfortable thought coiled in her stomach

like the timber rattlesnake she'd encountered on a trek through the forest. She shook off the memory. "Well, I need to go." She stepped toward the door.

Micah waved. "I'll give you a call when we organize the next fishing excursion."

"Thanks." In the parking lot, Madison clicked the key to open her car. Ryder's replacement at the store ranked high on her list of nice-looking men. But what difference did it make? She wasn't interested in Micah Collins, or any guy for that matter—not until the pieces of her heart mended.

The fairy-dust ringtone sounded on her phone. A text. Probably Ashton asking her to pick up something for the inn. She paused to read it.

Babe. Just checking on you. Hope you're okay. I'm sorry for the way things turned out. How can I make it up to you? Josh.

Madison firmed her lips. How dare Josh text her? She clicked off her phone and deleted the text. *You can make it up to me by not texting me anymore.*

Her stomach knotted into a tight ball. She didn't trust him. What was her ex-husband up to?

Micah watched the attractive woman as she walked out the door and trekked down the walkway as if she'd remembered a pending appointment. Her light brown hair swayed with her steps, and her soft blue eyes fascinated him. The flyrod incident had obviously been an embarrassment, and he felt a little sorry for her.

He wrote her name on a tag, attached the label, and

placed the rod in the stockroom. Then he straightened the rest of the rods on the rack. Madison Mitchell. Now he remembered. Ryder had mentioned her a couple of times last fall. Said he had a blind date with her once, and then they'd attended church together. But no more mention of Madison after Ryder began seeing Juliette.

He ran a hand through his hair. He needed to get back to work. Those new fishing vests weren't going to stock themselves. Yet, he thanked God every day for this job. His employment provided a roof over his head and food on the table. He couldn't live on his savings forever.

In the storeroom, Karina Soriano, Micah's assistant manager, unpacked a box of fishing lines and set the spools on the shelf.

"How ya doing today, Karina?" Micah set two large boxes on his cart.

"*Muy bien, gracias*. I'm fine."

"That's good to hear." The petite Hispanic woman had proven to be a good hire so far.

He rolled the two-wheeled cart to the clothing section in front.

On the next aisle, two women browsed through the display of sun visors. The first, dressed in tattered jeans and an old shirt that fit tightly around her belly, was around five months pregnant. She leaned closer to the second woman. "I don't care what my doctor says, I'm eating for two. Let's go grab a hamburger and fries in town. I can't afford any of these high-priced restaurants on the wharf."

The second lady grinned. "You've got another mouth to feed. My grandmother always said the same thing, and she had seven kids. After the burger, let's stop at the ice cream shop on Main. My treat."

Micah pinched his lips together. Eating for two. Misinformation that could prove harmful to a woman's health. Gestational diabetes wasn't worth the risk.

He shook his head and sliced open the box of vests with a boxcutter. He gave himself a mental kick in the pants and slid a vest onto a hanger. His work was here at Blake's store. The woman's health and the conversation between the two were none of his business.

Chapter Two

Sacramento, California

Jax Bates looked up. A smile crossed his face. What an unexpected surprise.

He stood as the beautiful blonde approached.

She blinked when she saw him. "Mr. Bates, how are you?" She didn't smile as she stood in front of his table at The Yellow Deli. She'd never been a very happy person anyway, and he could imagine why. Cancer stole the smile from so many, and it had stolen so much from him.

Jax motioned to the extra chair. "Victoria? Why don't you join me? We can catch up."

He really hadn't expected her to sit with him, but she did. After they placed their orders, he turned his attention to her. Though she was more than likely the age of their son, his wife, Mary had bonded with her throughout their treatments for cancer. "Did you ever wonder where Dr. Collins went after he ran from his practice here in Sacramento?"

Victoria eyed him over the edge of her drink, raised to her lips. "Why would you think that I even think about him?"

He gave her hand a fatherly pat. "My dear, Mary and I kept no secrets from one another. We were very close. She shared with me your infatuation with the good doctor."

Victoria leaned forward, closing her eyes. When she opened them again, she stared at him. "I find it strange that you would refer to him as a good doctor. You sued him, after all. Your settlement with his insurance company is probably the sole reason he left."

"Most likely, yes. And while I do believe that I deserved that settlement, I've had time to think about the past. They settled so I never got to hear Dr. Collins confess that he'd been responsible for Mary's death."

"She suffered an embolism, Mr. Bates. That was beyond his control. No matter how slight the surgery, the risks are always there."

Under the table, Bates tightened his fist and fought to keep from doing the same with his teeth. He forced a smile to curve his lips. "Yes. You're right. And as I was going to say, I have made it my goal to talk to Dr. Collins and to let him know that I no longer want him to pay for Mary's death. I did make some horrible threats against him at the time."

Victoria sat back. "How do you expect to find him?"

Jax smiled. "I have found him. I ran into the office manager for Collins' practice. He let it slip that the good doctor settled in Washington state. Research led me to what seems like a quaint little town called Cranberry Cove."

Victoria sat up a straighter but then seemed to

deflate. "He obviously doesn't want to be found."

"I believe that Mary set you up on a date with our son once, did she not?"

Wariness filled Victoria's eyes. "What did she tell you?"

"That Liam found you very charming, but you had eyes for only one person, and that person has been located in Cranberry Cove."

"I'm sorry that I made Liam feel that way. The truth is that Dr. Collins never reciprocated, but I can't deny that I haven't forgotten about him."

"Well, there you go. Seems both of us have a reason to trek to Cranberry Cove."

Victoria frowned, not taking her eyes off him. "Micah's been through a lot. His wife's death and your lawsuit against him. If he left Sacramento, he must need time."

"As I said, I see things very differently now. I got money for my pain and suffering—and no amount would be enough. I need to move on, and to do so, I need to tell Micah. What about you? Wouldn't you like to determine if he has moved on from his wife's death and if, perhaps, you have a future with him?"

She shook her head. "Mr. Bates, I was his patient, and I did get over-infatuated with him. I fell for him after the second appointment, but I never dreamed he could feel the same. I don't know if he knew how I felt about him."

Bates chuckled and shook his head. "He knew. Believe me. He knew. And I believe that when a man learns of a woman's care for him, whether he reciprocates or not, his feelings linger, but if you don't want to know, want to let the chance to find out slip by, that's your choice. I don't want to let the chance to apologize pass me by, though.

The server dropped off their sandwiches.

Bates took a healthy bite and then a sip of iced tea. "I do believe you're right. The lawsuit coupled with his wife's passing were more than he could bear. I don't want that weighing on him. Perhaps that will bring him back to practice in Sacramento where he's needed." He leaned back. "You believe he's needed, don't you?" He raised his brows.

Victoria didn't speak, and they ate in silence. Finished, she said her good-bye and headed to the counter to pay.

Bates watched her leave. His running into her here before his departure for Cranberry Cove was fortuitous. He didn't need her to do what he must, but should the seed he planted in her mind grow and bear fruit, he'd reap more satisfaction than he imagined he could.

Chapter Three

Two weeks after she signed up for fishing lessons, Madison clutched the expensive leather briefcase in her left hand and knocked at Ashton's office door with her other.

"Please, come in." Ashton's cheery voice made Madison's job at The Inn at Cranberry Cove more pleasant—defusing some of the pressure she endured with cranky guests.

She opened the door and smiled at the heartwarming scene before her.

Ashton sat in a chair to the side of her desk, her arms extended and palms open.

Baby Atwood, a delighted grin on his face, toddled toward her and squealed when he fell into her arms.

Madison set the briefcase on her desk and pulled up a chair. "He's so precious. You and James are blessed with such a beautiful child."

Ashton cuddled her toddler and turned to Madison with a look of wonder. "Our baby will never take the place of James's first little boy, but he helped to soothe his daddy's sense of loss."

"I was so sorry I couldn't attend your wedding."

"I totally understand. Your mother was ill." Ashton eyed the briefcase on her desk.

"Oh, I found this in the Philippians Room."

Ashton smiled. "Oh, yes. The room designated for guests who need to rejuvenate and rest. I'll give the guest a call today."

Madison probably needed to spend time in one of the rooms Ashton named after Bible verses. Her life felt the opposite of relaxed and confident.

"Ma." Ashton's baby leaned against her and cooed.

"Aww. How sweet." A part of Madison's heart regretted she'd never have a child. The Ashton's of the world could enjoy the privilege.

Ashton peered at her. "Madison, are you okay? You look as if you're concerned about something." She cleared her throat. "If you don't mind, what happened with you and Josh? You seemed so happy when you came to the Christmas Day gathering last year. You got married later, right?"

Madison uncrossed her legs and crossed them the other way. "I'm sorry I was so secretive—especially with you. I wish now I had talked things over with my best friend. Maybe my marriage wouldn't have ended in divorce—or perhaps I wouldn't have married at all."

Ashton held her baby with one hand and patted Madison's with her other. "I'm here now or anytime you need to vent. I'm sure divorce is hard."

Vent. The need loomed over her heart. Sharing with her friend always lifted some of the burden. "Josh and I eloped shortly after Christmas. I hate to confess that my motives weren't noble."

"What do you mean?"

Madison fiddled with her hands in her lap. She dared to meet Ashton's gaze. "The guy I thought I wanted to marry chose someone else."

"Ryder?"

Madison nodded. "I became interested in Ryder for the wrong reason. I thought the time had come, that I needed to be married. After all, my best friend had a husband and even a precious little baby."

Ashton clasped her chest. "Oh, Madison. I'm so sorry you felt that way. So, you didn't love Josh."

She fought the tears that threatened at the back of her eyes and shook her head. "No, but everybody else in Cranberry Cove was happily married. Blake and Gracie. Now Juliette and Ryder. I realize that marrying Josh was a foolish idea."

"What happened?"

Madison shook her head. "What happened was regrettable. We'd only been married a few months. In March, he started making excuses for why he couldn't come home in the evening, and then finally in May near the end of school, he left, sending me divorce papers. No explanation. Nothing. The last I'd heard, he'd moved to California with a waitress he met in Oceanview. Somehow, he managed to land another teaching position, though he quit his job here a couple of weeks early."

Ashton smoothed her hand over Madison's again. "I can't offer you an explanation of why these difficult things happened, but I trust the Lord to help you through this."

Madison didn't have time to listen to Ashton's talk about God. "A couple of weeks ago, I received a text—from Josh. He sounded sorry for what he did. I wonder if he wants to get back together."

Ashton lifted her brows. "You think you'll start a relationship with him again?"

"No way. I didn't answer, and I certainly don't plan to have anything to do with him—or any man for that matter."

"Hey, don't beat yourself up over your failed marriage. We all make mistakes." Ashton smiled. "Get up and go on. God has a plan for your life."

She didn't need to hear a lecture from her religious friend right now. "Have you heard from Juliette and Ryder?"

Ashton bounced her baby on one leg. "Yes. I got an e-mail from Juliette yesterday. She and Ryder are doing well. Ryder's picking up the language. She said her father is readying to retire, and he's basing it on Ryder's abilities to communicate in French."

Madison sighed. "I never dreamed they'd move to France."

"They should be home for a visit next Christmas. Ryder misses his parents."

She understood that. She hadn't seen her father for years.

"Speaking of Juliette, that reminds me. I have some news for you about the new chef."

Madison snickered. "I hope this woman doesn't have two thugs chasing after her like Juliette did."

"No. And the chef isn't a woman. Hold onto your chair."

"What?" Madison studied Ashton's face and her half smile.

"Tony is coming back."

Madison's mouth flew open. "You'd trust that egotistical cheat with your kitchen again? After he stole from you and caused you to fail inspection when the county inspectors came? Ashton, tell me you're kidding."

Ashton lifted her hand, palm up. "Hear me out. About four months ago, James and I saw Tony and his wife at church services. They were praying down front with one of the deacons."

Madison wanted to laugh, but she restrained her sarcastic reaction so as not to offend her friend. "I, er, — "

"I know what you're thinking. Merely seeing them in church was no reason to trust him again. As weeks went by, Tony and his spouse were there every week. One Sunday, they met us outside and asked for James's and my forgiveness. They'd asked the Lord into their lives. Shortly after, he gave us a check for what he owed us."

"Are you sure he wasn't trying to get his old job back?"

"He didn't ask for employment. James and I talked it over and decided to allow him another chance."

Madison rose from her seat. No doubt, Ashton would make the right decision. "I better continue cleaning rooms." She loved her friend, but Ashton's view of religion and hers were as far apart as one side of the universe to the other. Ashton spoke of her God, but to Madison, God seemed like some vague entity in outer space.

Madison quietly closed the office door and climbed the stairs to where she'd left her cleaning supplies. Ashton found what she wanted to do with her life—to run an inn and be a wife and mother. But what did Madison want? She'd only become a teacher because her mother and aunt encouraged her. She wasn't sure the profession was for her, but what was? And was it too late to refocus her life?

The last room clean and the living room vacuumed and dusted, Madison waved good-bye to Mrs. Mayberry and headed out the kitchen door to her car in the side parking lot. Three o'clock and the sun wouldn't set for hours yet. Shopping didn't appeal to her. Besides, she had little money to spare.

She took the highway into town. The sign on the side of the road reminded her. The state of Washington had recently opened the interior of the lighthouse to visitors. She could climb the spiral stairs for an outstanding view of the bay and the Pacific Ocean. Her pulse pounded a little harder as she passed the turn off for downtown and curved right at the entrance to the lighthouse.

After parking, she trekked up the path through old-growth forest. When the trees thinned, her heart skipped a beat.

The towering lighthouse she'd only seen in pictures materialized ahead. She drew closer to the building that seemed to reach to the heavens. She took a whiff of salt air. Seagulls gave their characteristic cries as several circled through the sky. Why hadn't she come sooner?

She approached the front door and stepped inside.

A woman sat behind a wide desk. "For the month of June, the lighthouse is free. Enjoy." She stamped the hand of the man in front of her and then looked up at Madison with a smile. "Here you go, ma'am." She pressed the logo of the lighthouse on the back of Madison's left hand. "Two more guests for now. Then I'll have to ask the rest of you to wait approximately fifteen minutes. We've reached the max number." She stamped the hand of the lady who'd been standing behind Madison and then that of an older man.

Whew, made it in time.

The guy in front turned and then chuckled. "Madison, Cranberry Cove's future fishing champ."

"Micah, the guy from the sporting goods store who's going to turn me into that champion. Hello." Madison clenched her jaw. Who cared if he made fun of her?

He grinned. "Care to climb the stairs with me? I understand the view from the top is spectacular."

Madison surveyed the spiral staircase. A long way up but she loved challenges. "Sure."

The stairs with only enough room for one curled around and up in endless circles.

Madison followed Micah as he took one step after another. He stopped at a landing with a window nook and peered out.

Madison stole a look over his shoulder. His woody scent delivered an unfamiliar impression to her stomach. What was that all about? She took a few steps back.

"I'm sorry. I was hogging the view." Micah stepped to one side. "The cape seems to blend into the ocean."

Madison smiled. "No problem." She leaned toward the window as the majestic scene took her breath away. Puffy clouds dotted the blue sky. White caps frolicked on the surface of the sparkling ocean below.

"Wait until we get to the outside platform. I've read that the landscape is like nothing you've ever seen before.

The man who'd entered behind Madison followed a distance behind as they climbed nearer the landing.

Micah glanced back. He widened his eyes, and then

he frowned. He took the stairs again.

Finally, at the top, she and Micah walked into the lantern room and then out the door and onto the platform.

The breeze swept Madison's hair into her eyes, and she brushed the stands behind her ears.

Far below, a sandy beach met emerald water. Beyond, waves looked like miniature ripples cavorting on the ocean's surface. At the horizon, puffy blue clouds melded with the ocean. "You're right. The view is outstanding."

Micah stood by her side. "Look at that ship. Seems strange the way the boat sinks below the horizon. If I didn't know the world was round, I'd think some giant monster swallowed it."

Madison laughed. "Like the sailors in Columbus's day."

The man and the woman, who didn't seem to be with him, followed them outside. They stood at the railing beside her peering at the view. Then the man glanced toward Micah with a slight smile. He held his hand out. "Hello, how are you doing? I've been looking for you." Are you here on vacation?"

Micah coughed and took a few steps toward the door. "I'm sorry. You must've mistaken me for someone else." He looked at Madison. "Shall we go back down so some other guests can come in?"

Madison nodded. "Yep, let's do it."

The man continued to stare at Micah as he made his way into the building.

After the climb down, Micah's frown only relaxed a bit. "I suppose I have a familiar looking face."

She stared at him a moment. Dark, kind eyes, which gave the impression he cared, seemed to focus on her.

And then he smiled. "Hey, friend, let's grab coffee soon."

"Yes, that would be fine." Madison allowed the words to emerge slowly. She didn't want a relationship, but somehow, she didn't think Micah was after anything but friendship. He didn't appear to be the flirty type. His quiet reflective eyes told her he merely needed a friend in Cranberry Cove. That perhaps he carried a burden he didn't care to share.

Micah climbed into his old Toyota he'd purchased before coming to Cranberry Cove. Driving his Mercedes would stir up questions about how he could afford one on his manager's salary.

He glanced in the rearview mirror in search of the man who'd approached him at the lighthouse, the last person he expected to see in the area. Bates. Why would he be here? And if he'd been looking for him, why? And how did he discover where Micah had moved?

Micah took the left turn to head to town and his apartment. He couldn't thank Ryder enough for recommending him to his landlord. Ryder's old place was small but adequate. He didn't need the extravagance of his large home in Sacramento.

Was he being followed? He rolled his eyes. Why would Bates do that? He hated Micah. He took a deep breath to clear his frustration. He prayed Bates would leave soon, and that no one in Cranberry Cove would discover who he really was.

Chapter Four

With her cotton cloth, Madison smoothed the linseed oil on the magnificent spiral staircase's railing. She rubbed the wood until the grains glistened. Since the elegant feature

served as the focal point when guests entered the inn, the structure should shine.

She exhaled a long breath. The old inn brought a sense of stability and security. To think, the lovely building had existed for years and remained a historical feature of Cranberry Cove. Some things didn't change, didn't abandon her. Like her father and later, Josh.

The front doorbell rang.

She descended the stairs and set the cloth and bottle of oil on the entry table. The bell rang again, and she opened the door.

A large bouquet of summer flowers hid the face of the person holding the crystal vase. A man leaned his head around the arrangement. "I have a delivery for Madison Mitchell."

Madison's heart pounded harder. "For me?" Who would send her flowers? She reached for the vase. "Thank you."

The man turned and headed toward the delivery truck with Cove Creations painted on the side, which he'd parked in front.

"Thank you, again," she called to the guy and waved.

Ashton walked down the hall from the kitchen. "Sorry, I heard the doorbell, but I had to finish up the inventory in the pantry." She glanced at the flowers in Madison's hands. "Who are those for?"

Madison gulped. "For me. I can't imagine who would send me flowers." Surely not Micah. She barely knew him. Madison set the vase on the living room coffee table and plucked the card from the plastic holder. She read aloud. "Madison, these flowers are to tell you how much I regret the way we parted. Yours, Josh."

"Josh? Are you serious?" Ashton ran her finger along the pedal of a delicate lavender dahlia.

Madison clasped her hands on her waist, the enchantment of receiving flowers gone. "Do me a favor and keep them here at the inn. I don't want them."

Ashton raised her brows. "Why? Do you suspect Josh may have ulterior motives for sending them?"

"I'm not sure. If he thinks we're getting back together, he's got another think coming."

Ashton centered the vase on the wide mahogany coffee table. "Well, if you're sure. I'd love to keep them here."

"Thanks. I don't trust Josh." She picked up her cloth and the bottle of oil and continued up the stairs again.

Ashton stood at the bottom. "Maybe he regrets what he did and wants to apologize."

"No. He's after something, and I want no part of it." Madison continued up and stopped at the landing. The beautiful stained-glass window Ashton's Aunt Gina had created never ceased to capture her attention. The sun shining through created a kaleidoscope of colors and portrayed the story Ashton had shared. A tale of two people who deeply loved each other—yet never had the opportunity to spend their lives together.

Longing welled inside, begging to emerge. Yearning to create a window like the one before her. How many times had she climbed the stairs and gazed at Aunt Gina's work of art? Today, the truth lodged in her heart. She wanted to learn to fashion beautiful works with stained-glass. Works of art which didn't wander away like an unpredictable, bored husband.

Madison finished dusting the stairs and returned to the dining room to clear any remaining breakfast dishes. From the first-floor window, she gazed into the backyard, beyond the deck. The small building caught her attention.

Ashton walked in from the kitchen. "Did I tell you how much I appreciate your help this summer? I'm going to miss you when you return to school in the fall."

Madison flashed a smile. "I'll miss seeing you and this country inn every day." She took a deep breath, reliving the awe she'd experienced only moments ago. She pointed out the window. "Did you say that your aunt worked on her stained-glass projects in that building?"

Ashton stood by her side and stared out into the backyard. "Yes, her studio. She created some amazing designs, which are now on display at an art shop downtown." Ashton paused. "I wish she'd made more."

Madison touched her friend's arm. "Would you consider allowing me to use the studio? I would love to learn the craft—as a hobby for now. I'd like to offer rent, but, honestly, I'm not sure where I'd find the extra money."

"Not a worry." Ashton's expression brightened. "I think it's a wonderful idea. I'd love to see Aunt Gina's studio in use again. What good is the building—sitting empty in the backyard?"

Madison clapped her hands. "Oh, thank you. I need to take a few lessons as well."

Ashton tipped her head to one side. "I believe the owner of the art shop offers instruction in the evening."

"Perfect." Did she dare to hope she could create the same quality pieces as Gina?

"There's very little left of her equipment, but you're welcome to what remains."

"You're the best friend anyone could have." She glanced toward the kitchen. "I better return to my duties, though, or Mrs. Mayberry will fire me."

Mrs. Mayberry glanced up from the cheese tray she'd prepared. "Madison, please take this to the buffet table in the dining room and then arrange the crackers on one side of the tray. There's a box in the pantry. Then come back for the fruit."

Madison found the crackers and placed the tray in the center of the antique, hardwood sideboard. An ornate vase held six glass calla lilies, no doubt Gina's works. A floor lamp with a leaded-glass lampshade sat at the other end of the room, bathing the area in muted light.

She reached for the sea salt crackers and opened the top.

"Well, hello. Did you enjoy the lighthouse yesterday?"

Madison turned toward the man standing at the door of the dining room.

The same man she'd seen yesterday adjusted his

glasses and smiled. "I loved the view from the top." He took a few steps toward her. "What about you and your boyfriend?"

She clasped her chest. "Oh, no. Micah's not my boyfriend. We only recently met."

"You were in good company then. Never hurts to have a friend who's in the medical field."

Madison frowned. The guy was obviously mistaken.

The man held out his hand to shake hers. "I'm Jax Bates. I took a room here until my cabin rental was ready. I know Micah from Sacramento. I'm sure if he thinks for a few minutes, he'll remember me." He cleared his throat. "He's a topnotch doctor."

"Micah?" Madison scrunched her brow. "I'm afraid that all the man you knew and the man here have in common is their first name. He's not a doctor. He's a manager of a fishing supply store at the wharf."

The man scrubbed a hand over his mouth. "Dr. Micah Collins… I'd know him anywhere, young lady. I'm sorry to disagree with you. He may not be practicing medicine here, but he did have a very successful practice in Sacramento, only a little over a year ago."

An attractive young blonde walked into the dining room and stopped. She started to back away.

"Victoria!" Mr. Bates clasped his hands together. "So, you did decide to see—let's say—the joyful sights in Cranberry Cove."

The woman seemed to blanch. "Yes, I did."

Mr. Bates pulled the woman forward. He glanced at Madison. "This is Victoria Brackenridge. She's one of Dr. Collin's former patients. She surprised me by coming, but we're both hoping to get a chance to visit with him while we're here."

Madison nodded with a smile. "It's nice to meet you. I hope you enjoy your stay at the inn." No way would she admit that the Micah Collins they sought was the same man she knew, though, it seemed more and more likely that he was. Why, then, had he denied that he knew Mr. Bates?

"I've read nothing but good reports about The Inn at Cranberry Cove." Mr. Bates lifted his chin. "I plan to tell our friends and business acquaintances in Sacramento."

Madison turned to the crackers again and spread them neatly on the tray. "I'll let you two enjoy lunch. Someone will be out to take your order soon." She returned to the kitchen and picked up the fruit tray which held slices of pineapple, fresh strawberries, orange slices, and kiwi and headed to the dining room again.

Mr. Bates and Victoria sat together at the table nearest the door to the deck. Victoria listened to something Mr. Bates said, nodding every few minutes.

Madison would love to eavesdrop but didn't want to appear rude. Maybe Micah was a doctor from Sacramento, but if so, why had he left his practice? Was he someone other than a manager of Blake's fishing store?

Micah waved at Karina who was vacuuming the lady's dressing room. "Will you be okay for a while? I'm going to the bank to make a deposit."

She looked up and turned off the vacuum. "I'll finish this later and keep an eye on the front until you return."

"That's fine. I'll be back before closing." He picked

up the deposit bag, slipped the paperwork inside, and climbed into his Toyota.

After making the store's deposit, Micah stepped outside into the sunshine, the weather perfect this time of year. He buttoned his jacket against the cool air and took a deep breath. Though he enjoyed running a fishing supply store in Cranberry Cove, Washington, he never dreamed he'd attend school for all those years and then work in a totally different profession.

He shook his head. *Lord, You know I'm grateful for this job. Forgive me for complaining.*

Micah strolled one block up the street where he'd parked the car. A familiar looking woman walked out of the art supply store. Madison.

He called out to her. "Hi, Madison. How's it going?"

She glanced up, and her eyes widened, almost as if she wasn't sure who he was. "Micah. How's everything at the store?"

He stopped in front of her. "Going good." The stained-glass pieces in the window caught his attention. "Back in high school, I tried making glass seagulls for my mom. My pieces left huge gaps."

She tapped his arm. "I'm sure they weren't that bad." She glanced toward the window. "The owner of Gianna's Glass Studio provides classes on all types of glass, mosaics, suncatchers, almost anything you can think of. I signed up for a basic class in learning how to use the tools."

"Sounds like a great hobby."

"Yes." She pointed to a butterfly wall-hanging. "I'd love to start working with glass. Ashton even offered me the use of her aunt's studio. As soon as I can get a little money ahead ... oh, I'm talking too much. What are you up to this afternoon?"

"Made a bank deposit." On a whim, he asked. "Would you like to go get that Starbucks?" An iced latte seemed a good idea before he returned to the store. He could use a friend right now, and Madison appeared to be a good listener with a great personality.

Madison paused, as if weighing the pros and cons. She nodded. "I could use a break—and I have something to ask you."

"Hmm. Okay. Let's get that coffee first."

At Starbucks, he set the two drinks on the table and pulled up a chair opposite the woman who had azure eyes and light brown hair. Attractive? Yes, but he couldn't afford to fall for anyone. Not even the lovely lady sitting across from him. Right now, he was curious to know the question she had for him.

Madison sipped her coffee and ran her finger over the whipped cream which covered her upper lip. "Aw, perfect."

"So, what question can I answer?"

She scratched her head. "Earlier today, I worked the lunch shift at the inn. That man who approached you at the lighthouse is staying at the inn for a day or so. He told me his name is Bates. He's from Sacramento. He said you were a doctor there."

Micah gulped a drink of coffee and then coughed. "I, er … " Bates, he'd hoped he wouldn't run into him again.

"But that's not all, Micah. A woman has checked into the inn as well. Though, she knew Mr. Bates, it was obvious she didn't arrive with him. She seemed embarrassed to have ended up in the same accommodations."

Micah remained silent. Who else in Sacramento had

sought and found him?

"Her name is Victoria. She's an attractive woman. Mr. Bates introduced her as your former patient—or another man named Micah Collins who looks like you and has a successful medical practice."

Victoria. He knew her well. Her temperament had been hard to forget, but what was her last name? Mary Bates had teased him that the pretty woman, his patient, had designs on him. He'd been married, and then he'd lost his wife. But he'd never have been interested in a patient.

"Micah? Are you a doctor from Sacramento?"

He pulled himself from his thoughts and nodded.

"Why the subterfuge? Are you in some kind of trouble?"

"I didn't want to advertise my former profession in Cranberry Cove. It's a long story."

"Look, Micah. If you'd rather not talk about it, that's fine."

"No. Frankly, I need someone to listen. I'd like to ask you to keep it quiet, although if Bates starts spreading the word around town, everybody will know."

"But why don't you practice medicine anymore?"

Micah drummed his fingers along the table. No hiding from Madison now. "Will you have dinner with me tonight at the inn? We can talk then."

"All right. I'll have Mrs. Mayberry add us to the reservation list."

Chapter Five

Micah glanced at his watch and splashed on some of his favorite aftershave. He ran a hand over his cheeks. Freshly shaven for once.

He needed to leave. Their reservations were in forty-five minutes. But was he ready to trust Madison with the difficulties he'd faced in the last several years?

Ryder's old apartment was fine except that he had to park his car on the street. He locked his apartment door—just in case. Ryder had said you never knew what might happen around this neighborhood. The guy had every right to express his concern as two men had showed up at his door once. Nearly beating him to death.

Micah made his way down the sidewalk to his car. "Oh, man. A flat tire." When he bought this clunker, he should've purchased new tires.

He popped the trunk and pulled out the spare. *Oh, no.* He scratched his head and frowned. The spare was as deflated as the other tire. Only one thing to do, but the decision wounded his masculine ego. He pulled out his phone and dialed Madison's number.

She picked up. "Micah, we said seven, right? I'll be on my way to the inn shortly."

He groaned. "I hate to ask, but could you stop by my apartment and give me a ride? I've got two flat tires."

She chuckled. "Sure. I'll be happy to. You still want to make dinner, or should I cancel?"

"Let's go to the eight o'clock seating. I want to drop off my tires at the service station on the way to the inn."

"I'm leaving now. Ryder's old apartment, right?"

"Yep." Careful not to mess up his clothes, he removed the flat tire and set it next to the spare. Now, he had to give his hands a good scrubbing.

The bell rang as he hunted for the heavy-duty soap.

Madison in a light blue dress that matched her eyes walked in. "I saw the two culprits outside by your car. Don't feel bad. I had a flat last month right before school ended. I couldn't find anyone to give me a ride so I walked." She ginned. "But my apartment is only a mile and a half from school."

Madison. As a single teacher, she likely watched her budget. Something he'd never had to worry about. Her humility and lack of pretense charmed him. He didn't know too many women like her in Sacramento.

He pointed to the couch. "Sit down and relax. I need to get this grime off my hands."

In the kitchen, Micah scrubbed his fingernails until all the grease and dirt had washed down the drain, and then he searched for a kitchen towel. After drying off, he headed into the living room.

Madison thumbed through a magazine, her brows furrowed. She turned a few more pages and wrinkled her nose.

Then he realized what she saw. The latest copy of his gynecologic oncology journal. Now she'd know for sure about his former profession.

She looked up. "You dealt with women who have cancer?"

He offered his hand to help her up. "Yes. I specialized in gynecologic oncology. I'll tell you more at dinner."

He hadn't thought about it when he'd asked her out, but he sure hoped Bates or Victoria didn't show up before he could offer Madison an explanation.

The scent of mustard, brown sugar, and apple cider vinegar emanating from Mrs. Mayberry's cordon bleu filtered in from the inn's kitchen. A different sensation circled in Madison's stomach. She couldn't wait to hear the explanation Micah had promised. Or could it be that a tall, very handsome man placed his hand on the small of her back as they made their way to the dining room? She tapped her forehead with two fingers. She'd sworn she wouldn't date again, but with Micah, things weren't romantic. She saw him as a new friend, and he likely felt the same about her.

At the entrance to the dining room, a waiter smiled. "Good evening." He offered them a table by the window overlooking the manicured landscape at the back of the inn and set two menus in front of them.

Micah's eyes lit as he glanced around at the elegant room. "Impressive. I imagine the food is delicious."

"Definitely. Juliette left many of her recipes with the inn and permission to cook them."

Micah took a sip of water from the long-stemmed glass in front of him. "Before we talk about me, tell me about yourself, Madison Mitchell." He grinned. "What do I need to know about you besides the fact you'd like to learn more about stained-glass and your casting skills need work."

She sighed. There were parts of her past she'd rather forget. "My life isn't exciting. I'm from Port Orchard where I lived with my mother until I left for college."

"Only you and your mom?"

"Yep. My father left us when I was nine. I have no idea where he is today."

He reached for her hand and then pulled his fingers back. "I'm sorry. Forgive me for asking."

She shook her head. "It's all right. His leaving happened a long time ago."

"So, how do you like working at the inn?"

A quick change of subjects, no doubt. "The job provides extra income. I'd like to begin taking lessons at the art studio downtown to learn how to make stained-glass projects. Stained-glass is a pricy hobby from what I understand."

The server arrived at their table.

"I don't need to look at the menu. Tonight's special should be delicious."

Micah handed his menu to the server, one of the college students Ashton had hired for parttime work. "I'll have the same, thanks."

Twenty minutes later, the server delivered steaming French onion soup laced with melted Gruyere cheese.

Micah looked at his bowl. "Do you mind if I say grace?"

Was he religious like Ashton? Well, it didn't matter if he said a blessing. "Please, do."

Micah's prayer sounded sincere and from his heart.

Not the memorized prayers she'd heard the few times she'd gone to church with her mother. At his amen, she lifted her head. "Did you learn to pray at home when you were a boy?"

"Yeah. My parents raised me to talk to God and read the Bible."

"I've never read much of the book." When was he going to tell her about the medical journal and his career as a doctor?

"I'll show you mine one of these days." He took a sip of his water. "But I think it's time to discuss what you saw on my coffee table and what Mr. Bates said."

Micah hesitated for a moment before venturing into his past.

Madison nodded, a frown on her face. "I'm listening."

Madison already knew his story. Now for the details. "I need to ask you to keep to yourself what I tell you."

"Of course. I wouldn't betray you. I understand what it feels like when someone breaks a promise."

The server set two plates in front of them. Asparagus in lemon butter sauce and double stuffed baked potato accompanied the healthy serving of the French chicken dish.

Micah glanced up and smiled. "Thank you. This looks delicious." No exaggeration there. He'd eaten at several French restaurants in Sacramento, and he figured the inn's cuisine would compare.

Madison squeezed lemon on the cordon bleu and

glanced up, no doubt ready for him to continue.

"Bates was right. I practiced medicine in Sacramento. An oncologist dealing with woman's issues." He took a deep breath.

"If I may ask, why did you leave your career for which I'm sure you trained for many years?" She squished her eyebrows together. "Managing a fishing store in Cranberry Cove has got to be a huge change. And you're too young to retire."

"You're right about that." He ran his finger around the rim of his water glass. "I put my practice on hold for now. For a number of reasons."

Madison twisted her napkin in her lap. "What reasons?"

"It's hard to explain. I got discouraged."

"With what?" She took a bite of asparagus and chewed. "I'm sorry. Am I asking too many questions?"

"No. No." His nerves relaxed. He needed someone to confide in. "I saw death more times than I wanted. Some of my patients died when I'd expected success— predicted the treatment would work well. I'd given hope to their families when there was none."

"But to quit a practice? Micah, doctors see patients die all the time."

He nodded. "I know. I don't want you to think I'm a coward or that I merely gave up because my patients passed away."

"But what else am I supposed to think."

Micah cleared his throat. He wanted to trust her. "All right. You deserve to hear the whole story." He placed his napkin on the table. "While still in undergrad school, I married my wife, Ellen."

Madison caught her breath. "But you're not married

now, are you?"

"No. Ellen died of bone cancer. Her doctor was a good friend of mine. He explored every avenue. He tried every treatment possible… " Micah's eyes stung.

Madison took a deep breath. "I'm so sorry."

"Around the same time, I'd performed a hysterectomy. The patient suffered a pulmonary embolism while under anesthesia. We couldn't save her. The hospital reported her death to the coroner, but his office determined I was not at fault." He rested his forehead in his two hands and then looked up. "Even so, the patient's husband decided to initiate a malpractice suit. That husband was John Bates. He calls himself Jax. That's the man who's in Cranberry Cove."

Madison shook her head. "How did it turn out?"

"My insurance company settled with Bates to avoid a costly and lengthy trial."

"I can't imagine the pressure you endured."

"That's not the end of the story." He took a deep breath. "The insurance company didn't settle right away. They wanted to test the merits of Bates' case. We went through preliminary filings, discovery, questions, depositions—and I had to prepare with the insurance company's attorney who represented me. I became inundated with paperwork, especially with the lawsuit." He paused a moment trying to compose himself. "Bates' lawsuit stole valuable time away from me and my wife during the last months of her life. I should've…" He guzzled a long drink of water.

Madison touched his arm. "I see how painful this is for you. You don't need to go on."

He pressed his knuckles into the palm of his other hand and squeezed. "Less than a year ago, Ellen died. I'd expected her to recuperate." He gritted his teeth. "Somehow, that didn't happen, and I was too busy with the absurd lawsuit."

Madison clutched his arm tighter. "I realize there's nothing I can say right now that would help."

He had to get to the whole truth. "After that, I had a couple of patients die, and I felt like I'd lost my wife all over again. Knowing I should've supported her when I didn't, those deaths became more than I could bear. I needed a break. I plan to return to my practice in the near future."

"So, you moved to Cranberry Cove. Do you have parents in Sacramento?"

"Yes, and they know where I am. They miss Ellen, too. I asked them to keep my location quiet for now, and they both agreed." He paused a moment, gazing into her eyes. "I needed to get away. Somewhere I could forget my past. A place where people don't know I'm a doctor. I saw Blake Sloan's ad on line, so I took the job working under Ryder." He crumpled the napkin in his fingers. "In Cranberry Cove, I enjoy the small-town atmosphere, the fresh air, the ocean. A place where I don't have to explain about my past to anyone."

Madison shook her head. "If word leaks out, I won't be the source."

"I trust you, Madison. I need a friend."

"Then I'll be happy to be one."

From the sincere look on her face, he knew she meant what she said. But how long would it take for Bates to spread the word? If Micah had to guess, his peaceful days had almost come to an end.

And what had brought Victoria to Cranberry Cove? Was it related to Bates or just an absurd coincidence?

Chapter Six

The next day, Madison patted her stomach, still full from the delicious French meal.

At the bottom of the stairs, Ashton shut the front door and thumbed through a handful of letters. "Hey, Madison. Would you like to look at the art studio?" She patted her pocket. "I found a spare key."

Madison descended the stairs, juggling the caddy with her cleaning supplies on one arm. "I'd love to."

"I need to speak to Mrs. Mayberry about next week's menu, so go ahead and check out the studio for yourself." Ashton passed over a keychain. "Hold the doorknob while you turn the key in the lock. Warning. It may be a bit dusty."

"No problem." She examined the keychain in her fingers. "Be still and know," was inscribed on a small piece of oak attached to the chain. Know? Whatever that meant, she valued the key and the studio for which it unlocked.

Madison set the caddy in the laundry room and walked out onto the deck. Though still cool out, the sun shone with a brilliance only found in Washington state. Even the thick leaves of the huckleberry bushes growing near the old studio reflected sparkles of light.

Holding the knob as Ashton said, she turned the key, and the door squeaked open. Though Ashton had obviously cleaned and straightened up since her aunt's death, the air carried a stale, damp smell as if no one had been inside for a while. She flipped a switch which covered the area in light.

Dust-laden work tables lined each of two walls. On each wall above the tables, Aunt Gina had attached peg boards. There was no sign of equipment except some hand tools and old gloves lying on a shelf. Madison's pulse pounded harder. This space was perfect for making art projects. But how expensive would the tools prove to be?

She returned to the inn and walked into the kitchen.

Ashton glanced up. "Hey, what did you think?" She wrote something on a clipboard and handed it to Mrs. Mayberry.

Madison drew both hands to her chest. "I'm thrilled."

Ashton waved for Madison to follow. "Come to my office. I want to ask you something."

A few minutes later, Madison sank into the chair on the other side of Ashton's desk. She couldn't imagine what her friend and boss wanted to say.

Ashton settled in an adjacent chair. "We've been friends since college. I hope you don't think me nosy, but what sparked your interest in stained-glass? The art became so dear to my aunt, and I never had the chance to ask her the same question."

Madison crossed her legs. "My mother dabbled in it when I was a child. Though our lives radically changed after my father left, her little flowers and glass fish and miniature frogs always remained on display in the window or on the kitchen table. I suppose the pieces represented permanence to me."

"I hadn't realized your dad left. You didn't mention your problems when we were roommates."

"I know. I didn't enjoy thinking of the past—and still don't."

Ashton leaned toward her. "I'm sorry you had a hard time then. With your husband leaving … "

Madison sat up straight. "I've learned my lesson. I can't depend on a man not to leave or betray me, but I can count on a gorgeous stained-glass work of art to adorn my home."

"Stained-glass breaks," Ashton whispered.

Madison's laugh sounded sardonic to her own ears. "Yeah, but I can create another."

"There is Another Who will never break and will never leave you."

"Now, don't get religious on me." Madison couldn't keep the sarcasm from her tone.

"I believe there'll come a day when you'll have questions about God." Ashton held up her hand. "But I'll say no more."

Madison smoothed her fingers over Ashton's. "Look, you are a dear friend. I know you mean well. I love you."

Ashton's smile said she wasn't offended. "Let me know if I can be of any help with glass making."

"Do you know how much starter kits run? I've read that they're expensive."

"I wish I could give you better news, but some can run as high as five hundred dollars."

Madison's stomach dropped to her shoes. She could never come up with that kind of money. She barely supported herself on her teacher's pay and the modest income she received from Ashton. She could get into stained-glass one small project at a time, but how long would that take? Could she dare to dream of opening her own studio someday?

On Saturday, Madison finished cleaning the inn's rooms, her duties finished for the day. She glanced out the back window at the studio, causing her pulse to drum in her chest. If only she could get started on a project. But she still needed to learn more of the technique before her first attempt. Oh well, at least she could unload the few basic supplies she'd purchased yesterday afternoon at Hobby House in Oceanview.

She made a trip to her car and returned with two large plastic bags and laid the contents out on the worktable. Inside the small space, she whirled around. Butterflies flittered through her stomach, and she clapped her hands. She had a studio and now a few supplies. She couldn't wait to get started.

The seven by ten sections of blue-green glass, the grinder, the soldering iron, and a few pliers sat like strangers on the workspace. Yesterday, the clerk at Hobby House in Oceanview had promised, "These items will get you started."

Madison picked up one of the glass pieces and lifted it to the light shining in from the window. The sparkling brilliant color reflecting on the wall sent tingles to her stomach. Now to learn how to turn this piece of glass into a work of art.

She placed the glass on the worktable. The fourth

inch section slipped, and she caught it with her other hand, slicing a nick on her finger. Good thing she followed the advice of the lady at the shop who said to keep band-aids on hand. She taped one around.

Someone tapped at the door.

Before she could answer, Ashton poked her head in. "Hey, Madison. I came to check on you. How are things going with the studio?"

Madison rested on a stool and pointed toward the other for Ashton to sit. "I can't remember a Christmas when I was this excited—even though I cut myself." She held up her bandaged finger.

"Oh, be careful. Aunt Gina said she did the same when she started." Ashton leaned toward Madison. "I have to admit, I had another reason for stopping in. I'm being nosy, but I wanted to ask you something. I meant to talk to you the day after the French meal, but it slipped my mind."

"You're my best friend. Ask away."

She snickered. "I had to stay late that evening to finish my kitchen supply inventory." She grinned. "I passed the dining room and saw you having dinner with some gorgeous guy. Tell me more."

Though Ashton was her friend, she couldn't—no, she wouldn't—tell her what Micah shared in confidence. "He's Ryder's replacement at Blake's supply store, Micah Collins. I signed up for fishing lessons."

Ashton giggled. "You weren't exactly taking a fishing lesson. I saw the way you looked at him."

"He needed someone to go with him to dinner." She bit the nail on her pinky. "He's only been in the area for about nine months and still doesn't know a lot of people. He's a friend."

"I've known you long enough to recognize that twinkle. You like him."

Madison clasped her hands on her waist. "Ashton Atwood. He's only a nice guy I met. I saw him at the lighthouse, and we walked to the top together. You know I'm not looking for another relationship." She needed to take the focus off the time they spent together.

A slow grin grew on Ashton's lips. "All right. If you say so."

Madison stood and glanced at the worktable. "Did you see my tools?"

Ashton rose and put her arm around Madison. "I did, and I'm so proud of you." She turned toward the door. "Gotta go. Love you."

Madison examined another piece of glass—more blue than green. Was Ashton right? Did she have a twinkled in her eye when she spoke of Micah?

Micah stifled a yawn and stuffed the fishing vest, waders, and a box of spinners in a plastic bag with Sloan's logo on the front. Then he handed the man his receipt. "Thank you for shopping at Sloan's Fishing Supplies." Tonight, he'd avoid reading his medical journal before bed.

The man stroked his beard. "Do you know where I can find a boat for rent?"

"Yes, there's a rental— " A chill traversed his spine, and an odd sensation jolted him. Something wasn't quite right. He glanced toward the customer again. "A few doors down, they lease fishing boats."

Movement toward the front window seized his attention. Someone shifted to the right and disappeared from view. Male or female, he couldn't be sure.

"Excuse me, sir." The customer leaned toward Micah and spoke louder. "Do you know if they provide guides?"

Micah blinked and then shook his head. "Er, yes, I believe so."

"All right. Thank you." The customer picked up his package and walked out of the store.

Micah followed him and stepped onto the wooden walkway. He looked to the right and then to the left. Nothing out of the ordinary. Merely Saturday shoppers and a few tourists perusing the wharf's stores. He scrubbed a hand over his mouth. His imagination ran wild when he didn't get enough sleep.

Inside the store again, Micah checked the notebook with people who'd signed up for fishing lessons as he had spare time tomorrow afternoon. Madison Mitchell's name appeared at the top of the list. He pulled out his cell phone and punched in her number. Maybe he could accomplish two things at once—take a customer to learn how to fly fish and enjoy the needed company of a friend. Maybe she'd even want to go to church first.

Chapter Seven

Micah by her side, Madison edged down into the pew nearest the back of the room he called the sanctuary. She wasn't sure why she'd agreed to go to church and told Micah she didn't want to sit any closer. When had she attended before? Once with Ryder last fall. And only so she could be near him.

Micah sat beside her and smiled. "Thanks for joining me. You'll like the service."

That's what he thought. Church made her nervous. She never understood why people gathered in the name of Someone who existed far away, a mysterious entity Whom many people had never heard of. How did they know God was real?

Ashton waved as she and James walked closer to the front and sat in the third row. Her dearest friend looked at her husband as if he were the most incredible man in the entire world. Another mystery. Did she actually love him that much, or had she fooled herself into thinking she did? Like Madison had misled herself in her relationship with Josh.

Madison stood with Micah as the crowd sang a few lively songs she'd never heard before. Then they sat when a man walked to the stage and sang a tune with words that confused her. Something about how a person would react when he saw God. Would he dance, or stand, or fall to his knees? Whoever wrote the song was convinced he'd see a Person named Jesus someday.

Finally, a man dressed in jeans and a casual green shirt stepped up on the stage and stood behind a podium with a microphone.

Madison poked Micah. "Is he the preacher?"

He smiled and nodded.

When the pastor asked the people in the room to open their Bibles, Micah scooted his toward her so she could read.

"Have you ever wondered if God is real?" The preacher looked up with a smile. "I believe if we're honest, all of us have. Romans 1:19 says: 'What may be known about God is plain, because God has made it plain. For since the creation of the world, God's invisible qualities—His eternal power and divine nature have been clearly seen, being understood from what has been made, so that people are without excuse.'"

What things did the Bible refer to? Things like the stars and moon? Or perhaps the mountains and forests. Maybe she'd ask Micah after church.

Later, the pastor said some kind of closing prayer and people began to walk out of the church.

In the hall in front, Ashton strolled by with a wink and a wide grin.

Madison would set her straight Monday. This outing with Micah meant nothing other than she'd learn to fly fish.

Micah stopped the car at the parking lot and glanced at Madison in the passenger seat. "Wildhorse Mountain Lake is new to me, but the basic tenets of fly fishing are the same in most areas."

"The walk to the lake is only a half-mile." Madison's gazed out the front window. "The view is spectacular from the lake's banks. The snowcapped mountains, the trees… do you suppose the preacher meant lakes and fir trees and beautiful skies when he read those words from the Bible?"

"You're referring to Romans 1 and verse twenty where he says people don't have an excuse for not believing in God." Micah got out of the car and secured his fishing equipment from the backseat.

Madison grasped the picnic basket she said she'd prepared before church. "Yeah, that's the one. I got confused."

The familiar chirp of a chickadee echoed through the trees. Micah weighted his words as he walked by her side and followed a downhill trail to the lake. "Yes, the passage is saying that people who've never heard about God can know Him by what He's created. Like the birds we hear now. No man could've created what we observe in nature and especially out of nothing." He smiled at her. "You've got the right idea about what the Bible is telling us in that passage." If he could encourage her, he would.

Throughout the service, Micah had caught glimpses of Madison's face—during the singing, the praying, the preaching. No doubt, she wasn't bored, but her expression seemed to indicate she'd never heard those concepts before. He blew out a breath. Now he understood the strong urge to pray for her yesterday. She needed to know the Lord.

At the edge of the lake, he helped Madison step into her chest-high waders over her jeans, trying to avoid gawking at her womanly curves. "This is the best spot. Where the stream flows into the lake." He led her into two-foot-deep water.

"How did you learn to fish?" Madison adjusted her pony tail through the back of her ball cap.

"My dad used to take me out all the time when I was a teenager. There're a lot of spots for fishing around Sacramento."

"How come we only have one pole?"

He grinned at her many questions. "This one is the one you purchased. Don't you recognize it?" he teased. "I'm going to help you learn to use it."

He sloshed behind Madison and slid the handle into her hand, savoring the feel of her smooth skin. "You flick your wrist a few times through the air and then cast out your line onto the water's surface." He guided her hand as the fly met the water. "The current will straighten the line."

A soft breeze blew in his direction, encircling him with her fresh, flowery fragrance. "When a fish hits, jerk the line back, like this." His hand on her smaller one, he demonstrated the motion. "Okay, are you ready to try it on your own?"

Her grin seemed almost childlike. "I think I'm getting the hang of this, but maybe you should stand back so I don't whack you again."

He laughed and waded to the bank to retrieve his pole and equipment.

After thirty minutes of casting, Madison caught three fish, and he'd only had one bite. He hollered to her about ten feet away from him. "Hey, you're a pro. Proud of you."

She glanced up to where they'd walked from the parking lot. She motioned with her finger and lowered her voice. "Micah, look over there."

He followed the direction she pointed.

At the edge of the parking lot, in the middle of foilage, a man in jeans and a black hoodie stared through binoculars in their direction.

A chill worked its way down Micah's back. The guy wasn't a game warden. Wasn't dressed in a uniform. Who knew what the creep was after?

The man lowered his binoculars and waved. "Sorry." He made his way toward them along the shore.

Micah lifted his arm and stepped in front of Madison. "Stay behind me."

"You don't think he's dangerous?" she uttered.

"We're deep in the woods, Madison. What I think isn't relative. We always need to be cautious."

The man stopped on the shore in front of them. "I didn't want you to think I was spying on you." He gave a laugh that came with a deep rumble. "I'm scouting out a place to fish."

"With binoculars?" Micah challenged.

The man laughed again. "I deserve that. I suppose it was a little unsettling to see a man looking down your way with a pair of binoculars. Truth is, I hike, and I've learned that a good pair of binoculars can keep you aware of any approaching danger—like a bear. Then I saw the little lady doing such a good job of fly fishing, I wanted to study her technique. Name's Ford." He raised his hand.

"In fact, I've seen the little lady before." He nodded in Madison's direction. "I'm staying at the inn. You work there, right?"

Madison remained silent.

"Well, look, I'm sorry I encroached on your day out." He started to make his way back the way he'd come.

"Mr. Ford?" Micah called. "Where's your fishing equipment?"

Ford stopped and turned. "I'm scouting today. Tomorrow is for fishing." He waved and moved on.

"Let's call it quits. We can come back next week." Micah patted the holster with the concealed weapon in his back pocket. He never came out here without it. If the man meant harm, he was ready to protect Madison.

Madison studied Micah's pinched lips and slight frown as he drove down the mountain toward Cranberry Cove. Something about the man with binoculars gave her the creeps. He'd said he was staying at the inn, but she hadn't seen him. She kept that to herself.

Micah didn't say anything, but she figured he felt the same because of his insistence that they leave the area.

Or maybe both she and Micah were overly cautious.

When they hit the main road, the lines in Micah's face smoothed. "Are you sure you haven't fly-fished before?"

She laughed. "Honest. Other than when I was a kid, no."

"You have a good memory. Next time you come in the store and try out a rod, I don't think you'll knock me in the head."

She nestled into the seat and exhaled a long breath. Spending time with Micah felt relaxing. She didn't have to fight for his attention or keep her fingers crossed that he'd listen to what she needed to say. So different than Josh. "Other than dangerous women who don't know how to handle a fishing rod, do you like your job at the store? I'm sure it's different than your former profession."

"True. I've always liked outdoor sports. When I learned Ryder was leaving and Blake promoted me, I gladly accepted." He switched on the radio. "You dated Ryder for a while?"

"For a while after Ashton wanted to arrange a blind date with him."

"If you don't mind me asking, why didn't it work out?"

"I don't really enjoy talking about it, but you might as well know. I appreciate that you've been transparent with me."

He glanced at her and back to the road. "I believe in honesty."

"I'm reluctant to tell you, though. Your opinion of me may not be the same." She enjoyed the rainbow of colors from the wildflowers blooming along the road a moment more and then tensed her shoulders. "I was in love with the thought of marriage. In fact, I got married in January."

"This last January?" His eyes widened. "Are you telling me you're married?"

She patted his arm. "No, Micah. Not anymore. My husband filed for a divorce after only three and a half months. Our marriage was dissolved about a month ago. But he left well before filing."

"I don't make a practice of hanging out with married women, so that's a relief."

"Trust me. I wouldn't have gone to dinner with you if I was."

"I'm sorry." He swiped a hand through his hair and slowed as the road curved through the thick forest. "No one is immune to problems with the opposite sex. Including me."

What had he meant? Did he have a girlfriend who dumped him at some point in his life?

Chapter Eight

Madison smoothed a dab of aloe on her nose. Had she worn her straw hat with the protective wide brim yesterday at the lake, she wouldn't have burned her skin. Yet catching more fish than Micah made her smile. He was supposed to be giving her lessons. Maybe he should take a few from her. She chuckled with her silly thoughts.

She removed the soiled linens on the breakfast tables and replaced them with clean ones. In the laundry room, she tossed the tablecloths in the large white basket.

Instead of Mrs. Mayberry in the kitchen, Tony mixed cooked chicken, mayonnaise, celery, and pickle relish in a large bowl. Six loaves of multigrain bread sat on the counter.

Madison took a few steps in his direction. "Tony, it's been a while."

Tony looked up from stirring the ingredients and smiled. "I understand you're working at the inn this summer."

Something about his eyes had changed. She couldn't define the difference. "The last time we were in this kitchen together, I wasn't supposed to be here." She laughed. "Don't worry. I'm legal now."

"I remember." He added chopped pecans to his mixture and stirred. "You asked if you could make yourself a sandwich, and I told you yes. Should've said to wait in the dining room while I made it. We caused Ashton some problems that day. I'm grateful she has a forgiving heart."

Madison ran a hand through her hair. "A lot of things have changed since then."

"Including me—in a way I'd never have predicted." His face flushed with a glow.

"Oh?"

"For one thing, I'm a dad now." He set bread slices on a tray and placed a scoop of chicken mixture on each. "My wife and I are totally in love with our little girl."

"Congratulations." *Let's see how long that lasts.* Madison's mother had often said she'd thought marriage was forever. Somehow that didn't happen in the Mitchell household. Hopefully, Tony wouldn't abandon his wife and child.

"Did Ashton tell you we're attending her church?" Tony spread the chicken on the bread using a utensil with a round, serrated blade.

"She did. What changed?" The minute she spoke, she regretted her words. Now she'd have to listen to some kind of sermon.

"I got what I deserved when Ashton fired me for lying and stealing from her. My wife was sick—on bedrest because of a difficult pregnancy. I got kicked out of culinary school."

Madison folded her arms over her chest. "Sounds rough."

He nodded. "I searched for something or Someone to

help get me out of the jam I'd made. I came to the end of my resources. I had nowhere to turn so I looked up."

"To God?" Not quite the sermon she'd expected.

"Yes." He set the spreader on the counter. "I learned that I couldn't do life without Him, without a Savior." He smiled.

She turned to leave. "I'm happy for you." Maybe God felt sorry for him because Tony had found himself in so much trouble. But God wouldn't take pity on her, she was sure.

Monday afternoon, Micah turned the open sign to closed and locked the door to the fishing supply store. An image of a man with binoculars staring at him and Madison had jarred him awake a couple of times last night. Despite the man's approach to explain, Micah's overly active imagination played with his mind. He'd never seen the man before yesterday. He had no reason to suspect him of anything but what he'd said. Micah needed to put the incident out of his head.

His car remained in the spot where he'd parked early this morning. Visions of pouring a cold glass of iced tea, kicking up his feet, and not thinking about the inventory of fishing spinners he needed to finish tomorrow sounded good.

He twirled his car keys in his fingers and hummed a tune he'd heard at church. What would he have for supper tonight?

"Dr. Micah Collins." Someone with a deep voice spoke behind him. Someone who knew his identity.

Micah swiveled around and then did a double take.

"Bates. What are you doing here?"

Jax Bates smiled a wide grin. "Micah, I need a moment to talk to you."

"Didn't you express all you needed to say in pleadings for the lawsuit your lawyer filed against me?"

The man, glasses propped up on his nose, rubbed the back of his neck. "I've changed my thinking since then." He extended his palm toward Micah. "Look, can I take you to dinner. I only need a little of your time."

Micah restrained the urge to scoff at the man, this one who'd brought a malpractice suit against him and who had stolen precious time from him and Ellen. The one whose lawyer accused Micah of sheer negligence. What could he possibly want to say?

Bates lowered his eyes. "I understand how you feel. I had a tough time after Mary died. She was the love of my life, and I was empty without her. In my despair, my grief, all I could think of was who to blame. You were the easiest target."

"Well, the settlement did nothing to prove that I didn't act negligently."

"Now that time has passed and my grief has ebbed, I see what I've cost you. And I want to square things with you."

Micah stepped a few feet closer to his car. He couldn't imagine Bates meant what he said. The man was up to something.

Bates rubbed his chin. "Please give me a chance to explain. I'm a different man now." He laid a hand on Micah's shoulder. "I got to thinking. You suffered the same kind of heartache I did when your wife died. I can't imagine how you must've felt losing a spouse and dealing with a court case at the same time." He studied his feet. "Look, man. I need to say how sorry I am to have caused you the extra pain."

Micah narrowed his eyes as he stared at Bates. "I have to admit I never thought I'd hear those words from you, but you've said them. I accept them. You can leave."

"I came to Cranberry Cove to make amends with you. Can we at least not hold animosity against each other. Say you'll forgive me."

Micah's mouth dropped open. Forgive? The Lord commanded he forgive others. Wasn't accepting an apology the same thing has forgiveness. He pressed his lips together for a long second, thinking. No, he needed to say the words to the man, no matter Bates' intentions. "Sure, Bates, of course. I forgive you. I'll always regret what happened to your wife. But if it's any comfort to know, before we're born, God knows the number of our days."

Bates held up his palm. "All right. And thank you for allowing me to clear the air."

"Yeah." Micah climbed in his car. In a million years, he'd never have believed that Bates drove to Cranberry Cove to reconcile with him. But he had no other choice but take the man at his word.

Micah looked in his rearview mirror and then blew out his cheeks.

Mr. Bates waved, a pleasant smile on his face.

Micah couldn't help but lift a prayer to God that Bates would leave Cranberry Cove.

62

Chapter Nine

When his assistant manager walked out of the storeroom, Micah glanced up from stocking wool socks on the display table. "How was your evening last night?" A little more peaceful than his, he hoped. His attempt at a deep breath failed. He still couldn't believe Bates had meant what he said much less traveled almost seven hundred miles to tell him.

Karina must've missed a few nights sleep given the dark circles under her eyes. "I fixed a big Mexican fiesta for my family—enchiladas, tacos, Chile rellenos, refried beans. I want to cook for them while I … " She gazed toward the store's front window. "Most of my family drove over from Oceanview. We played cards and sang our favorite Spanish songs. How was your evening?"

"Fine, thanks." He straightened the fishing rain jackets hanging on the rack. Why tell her an old foe showed up? And then last Sunday, someone with binoculars spied on him and Madison at the lake. Not some birdwatcher, but a person who scrutinized them. Not only that, someone had stared at him through the store's windows the day before. Karina might think him paranoid.

The front doorbell rang, and Karina glanced toward the front. "I'll get it, Micah." She grinned. "Or maybe I should let you wait on the customer. A beautiful blond lady in a fancy dress just walked in."

He looked up from the rain jackets to the store's entrance. "I'll see to her."

The woman with flaxen hair flowing halfway down her back smiled at him. "Micah. I'm glad to see you. How are you?"

No way could he mistake the identity of the lady with a lowcut dress and spiked heels. "Victoria. I heard you were in town, but why are you here?"

She strolled around the store, shoulders back, examining every rack of clothes. "Your store looks well cared for. So typical of Dr. Collins. Perfection." She whirled around. "When Mr. Bates mentioned that he'd discovered your location, I thought I'd come and see how you're doing?"

No doubt, Victoria's father, Sacramento's wealthiest lawyer, footed the bill for her trip here.

"But why would a patient seek out a doctor who isn't practicing any longer?"

She turned toward him, determination in her move. "Why did you leave Sacramento?"

"Long story. I took a break from practicing medicine." He didn't have the time or energy or the obligation to explain things to her. He motioned her to follow him into his office.

She edged down into a chair and crossed her legs. Leaning forward, she rested both hands on her knee. "I'm glad to see you're well. After you left Sacramento, I realized how much I missed you. Merely knowing you were close brought comfort."

Micah dropped down in his office chair. "There are other good doctors available in Sacramento."

"I wasn't referring to you as a doctor, but as a friend. After my surgery, you comforted me in a way no other did. Only you could appreciate what I endured."

Micah shook his head. "Any gynecologist would've done the same."

"You don't understand, Micah. As I said, I considered you a friend. I hope you feel the same about me, that you'd be worried about me if I vanished off the face of the earth."

"You were my patient, Victoria, nothing more. I'm sorry if you thought our patient-doctor relationship was anything but that."

She sat silent for a long moment while Micah watched her face. The soft lips of sadness morphed into a hard line. "I'd hoped that we can become more than friends."

Micah stood and paced the room a few times.

"Have you seen Mr. Bates yet?" she asked. "He really wants to apologize to you for what he put you through."

Victoria, as Micah recalled, had been a friend of Mary Bates, bonding with the older woman during their treatment. Victoria had also been very impressionable, almost gullible to a certain extent. Micah supposed that she could have remained friends with Bates after his wife's passing. And now, she repeated what Bates had said about his reasons for seeking out Micah. Could he actually have changed?

Victoria stood and met him on one of his trips to the opposite wall. "I'm here because I care for you." She searched his face, as if looking for some kind of answer. "I'll always be grateful to you for helping to restore my health. Now I want to be by your side. To befriend you in any way I can. If a relationship is in our future, I wouldn't rule it out."

He had no feelings toward this woman, never had, nor would he ever—not even as a friend. In the little bit of interaction they'd had during her treatment, he knew her to be a spoiled rich girl, capable of great wrath if she didn't get her way. Her parents had always danced lightly around her.

He had to walk a thin line to avoid her retaliation. "Thank you, but right now, I'm fine. Living here in Cranberry Cove has given me a new start. No one knows me here—except those Bates spoke to about my identity. Life is peaceful."

"You don't miss your job or your old friends?"

"For now, I'm getting a new start. Have you sought out a support group where you could share with others who've undergone the same surgery?"

Victoria poked out her lower lip like a rebellious child.

Micah feared a tantrum might be on the horizon, and he didn't think the store could withstand it.

"Yes, but none of the groups help me feel better about myself." She placed her hand on his arm. "There's something about a doctor-patient relationship. You're the only person who truly understands."

Micah slipped down behind his desk as if it were a fortress between him and her. When Ellen was alive, he'd endured enough of Victoria's neurotic behavior. She'd passive-aggressively come on to him every chance she got and storming out of his office more often than not.

She tossed her shiny, straight hair so the strands swirled around her cheeks. "Can't we at least go to dinner? The seafood restaurant a couple of doors down looks fabulous."

Micah stood, his arms crossed over his chest. "I don't want to discourage you from enjoying your vacation, but I can't go to dinner with you." No way he'd use dating Madison as an excuse. Victoria was staying at the inn and would likely see her, perhaps attempt to talk about him with Madison. "Right now, I need to take a break from my past. But there's a wonderful seaside town up the coast called Oceanview. Visit MarineWorld." He strode to the door and opened it.

She narrowed her eyes at him. "I plan to stay awhile. In a few days, when you see things differently, you'll call me. Would you at least walk me to my car?"

"Sure." He followed her through the door and out to an expensive red car. "You rented a Porsche?"

"Yes, of course. There's a great company in Oceanview." Victoria sat in the driver's seat and rolled down her window. "I hope you'll call."

Micah rested his hands on her open window. "I hope you'll enjoy yourself while you're here."

She rolled up the window and squealed her tires as she pulled out of the parking lot.

Micah stared after her. If Bates encouraged her to come, and he probably had, what were her real motives for being here? And what about Bates? Had he really wanted to make amends? Or did he have a plan of revenge mapped out? Micah would likely find answers in the near future.

The long days of summer suited Madison fine. More daylight after work to do whatever. With the crowded downtown streets, she parked a few blocks from the art store. Her first stained-glass lesson and the teacher had asked her to come early. Her insides romped like a child out of school for the summer.

She passed a store on the way to the studio and then stepped back. In the window, plaques and wall-hangings were displayed among several books including the Bible.

A plaque with a floral background featured familiar words. "Be still and know that I am God."

She paused at the window and read the words again. They were similar to the ones on the keychain Ashton had given to her. Now the words on the keychain made more sense with the addition of the entire phrase. God could be known if a person would be still. Or something like that.

She frowned and read the plaque again. Why did she need to remain calm and quiet? Maybe to take time—to think about the things He'd made.

Madison turned toward the art studio. All the thoughts about God stumped her. Talking to Tony, another puzzle. At first, she dismissed his story, yet no doubt, the man had changed. Had the chef sat still and figured out who God was? If his God could've made that huge a difference in Tony's life, maybe she should know more about Him.

The one person she trusted for answers was Micah Collins. She'd ask him the next time she saw him.

Chapter Ten

After her lesson, Madison returned to her car. The words on the plaque circled in her brain. The message wasn't merely well-written or poetic. "Be still and know that I am God" meant more. More than an ordinary adage because the words spoke of Someone eternal.

Downtown afternoon traffic had picked up. When a break in the cars came, she pulled out from her parking spot and onto the main road.

Mom's birthday was only a couple of weeks away, and the shops at the wharf offered unique gifts. Besides, maybe she'd see Micah and get a chance to ask the questions which still remained unanswered.

She turned off the ignition in the wharf parking lot and took the steps to the new shop she'd spotted a few weeks ago. Inside Sea and Sand, she picked out a pair of gold earrings in the shape of seagulls. Perfect. A little expensive, but Mom needed to know how much she loved her. She tucked the little package in her purse and walked outside.

Madison glanced toward the parking lot and spotted her car. And then she blinked.

A few rows down, Micah leaned on the window of an expensive car, both elbows resting on the side.

A woman with long blond hair who could've given Miss America competition sat in the driver's seat of an expensive Porsche.

Two heads moved closer as Micah and the woman seemed involved in some kind of conversation. Had he taken up with a girlfriend since his wife died?

Madison focused a few seconds longer and then realization hit. He was talking to Victoria, the woman from Sacramento who'd sought out Micah.

Madison marched to the other end of the walkway. No sense in running into Micah now. She blew out a breath. She and Micah had made no promises. In fact, they weren't in any kind of romantic relationship. Only friends. Isn't that what she'd told Ashton? Isn't that what she preferred? Micah could talk to anyone he wanted.

So why had a lump lodged into her throat, and her heart shrunk to nothing?

On the opposite end of the parking lot, about fifty yards away, another figure walked nearer Micah and the woman.

Madison held her breath. The man they'd seen at Wildhorse Mountain Lake, this time with no black hoodie—but he was carrying the same set of binoculars.

The man lifted the binoculars to his eyes and turned them to roam the area. His perusal hadn't landed on her yet. Then he took a few steps under the wharf and out of view.

Micah walked back from the car as the blond drove away.

He needed to know that Ford had been watching him here. Ford had lied to them. The sooner she could talk to

Micah, the better.

When the bell over the front door dinged, Micah looked up from the cash register to the front door. Surely not Victoria again. Though he felt compassion for her, he'd never be interested in her. Her worldliness didn't appeal to him.

Madison stepped inside, no smile on her face. Something seemed wrong. What—he had no clue.

Karina glanced at him from stocking women's tee-shirts. "I'll take care of her, Micah."

He walked out from behind the cash register. "No, that's all right. She's a friend."

Karina chuckled. "Sure got a lot of nice-looking lady friends. I'll be in the stockroom if you need me."

He frowned. "Lady friends?" Then he remembered Victoria had visited the store a little earlier. He couldn't help his grin. "It's not what you think, Karina." He approached Madison. "This is a surprise."

Madison took a few steps toward him. "I'm sorry to bother you, but I need to talk. Do you have a break soon?"

Micah glanced at his watch.

An older lady strolled in and sorted through the spinners. "I need to take care of her." Dinner time approached, and his stomach growled. "Can you meet me at the Wharf Seafood Restaurant in an hour?"

Madison frowned as if she wasn't sure or couldn't wait that long. "Okay, I'll see you then." She grasped his shoulder. "Be careful on your way there."

What could she mean? "Sure. I'll try not to fall off the railing or into the ocean." He laughed.

His joke didn't change her expression as she walked out the door. "Make sure you're not being followed."

No time to ponder what she said as the customer moved from spinners to the far wall. The woman with graying hair sorted through the rack of fishing vests and then took one off the hanger. She turned it over several times in her hands and then held it to her cheek.

"May I help you with something," Micah said.

"Oh." She jerked her head up as if startled. Her eyes were red and a tear slipped down her face. "No… I—I'm sorry."

"Can I help you find another brand? You appear to be upset." Micah glanced at the rack adjacent to the first one.

She picked up the hanger and replaced the vest on the display. "This kind was my husband's favorite. He was an avid fisherman." She shook her head and stared at her feet. "You see, I come in here on occasion. Somehow your store helps me to remember my spouse before he got sick. He had cancer."

The sympathy he'd always held for others who'd experienced the ravishes of the cruel disease came rushing back, submerging him under a wall of turbulent water. "Ma'am, I'm sorry. You take your time. I'll leave you, and should you need something, let me know."

A light gleamed in her eyes, as if another's sympathy lifted a fraction of the burden.

When Karina returned to the front of the store, Micah strolled to the storeroom with the magnificent view of the bay and the water. With the sun lower in the sky now, the rays stretched across the ocean in a long, silver streak. He stared out the window, but the woman's grief filled his mind and lingered in his heart.

He'd seen that pain before in the faces of family members and spouses who's loved ones hadn't made it—who'd died from the disease Micah was supposed to cure.

As if he'd heard Someone speaking to him, he understood the message. *You can still make a difference.*

Micah gazed at the ocean. In the past, the Lord had spoken to him, but from His Word, the Bible. Could God be nudging him? "How, Lord?" he whispered.

Comfort those who remain.

A tingle ran along Micah's spine. As a sponge expands when filled with water, so understanding saturated his heart. Comforting those who were left behind after the loved one passed would offer service to God.

A seagull soared through the sky to sail beside another, and then the two landed side by side and perched on a piling. If God could direct two birds through the atmosphere, He could speak to Micah. Yes, Micah knew what he had to do.

Not all Micah's patients had died. In fact, the majority had survived. He'd successfully treated many women with breast and cervical cancer. But now he could do more. But how did he go about carrying out God's plans?

Madison. She was a good listener. Though she might not have the same connection to the Lord as he, she'd have ideas. He could brainstorm with her.

Out the restaurant's window, the sun crawled toward the horizon. Madison gazed out at the ocean, the sun's beams cavorting on the still waters. A quiet dinner with Micah sounded wonderful, but at the same time, she needed to tell him about the man with the binoculars. She took a sip of ice water from the pale rose goblet. Though curiosity nudged her to ask questions about the woman in Micah's car, she didn't want to appear nosey.

"Madison, thanks for getting a table." Micah slid in across from her, his woodsy scent exhilarating.

She breathed deeply and secretly wished she could move closer. A light sprinkling of whiskers covered his cheeks, and his piercing eyes fixed on her.

An expression she found hard to read settled across his face—perhaps one of admiration or awe. "I have an idea. I believe there's something more I could do to help those impacted by cancer—other than medical treatment."

"So, you don't plan to go into practice again?"

"Yes, I do, but I'm referring to a possible ministry in Cranberry Cove. The families in this area who've lost loved ones need support." He tapped his chest. "I'd like to provide that help in some way if I can."

Madison took a deep breath. "I love the idea. What about a place where people can go to find comfort when they need it the most? Merely having another who will listen—conversations with others who've faced the same hardship. Counseling services of some kind."

Micah's smile cheered her. "Exactly. A local center that's open in the evening hours, or on the weekend. Perhaps we could call it The Caring Center."

"But where would you find the funds to buy a place like that? And who would man it?"

"One thing at a time," he laughed. "Campaign churches, charities, people in the community. Organize a non-profit. Seek volunteers. It could work."

"If you're serious, I'm in. I'll be happy to do what I can. I know what it feels like to lose a parent. Though I assume he's still alive somewhere on this earth, my father died to me all those years ago."

Micah's face was filled with an inner glow. As if some of the pain he carried had lifted.

"Thank you, Madison," he whispered.

The server came to the table to get their drink order and left.

Madison gazed out the window again, and then the blond in the Porsche filtered into her mind. Had Victoria given him the idea to help families of cancer victims? "I suppose the beautiful woman I saw you with in the parking lot sparked your interest in this project."

"What? You saw me with her?"

"Yes, today after I left Sea and Sand."

Micah frowned and then shook his head. "No. I told you, Victoria is a former patient. Actually, a customer in the store gave me the idea."

"I see." Surely, he wouldn't mislead her about the blond and his relationship with her. And why would he want to?

She attempted to ignore her pulse which tapped a fast rhythm in her chest. "I hated to barge into your store today, but something happened that you need to know about."

Micah sat up straight. "Madison, I'm sorry. You wanted to tell me something. You said to be careful on my way here."

"I'd forgotten with all the plans you want to make."

She gripped his fingers. "Ford, the man with the binoculars we met Sunday when we went fishing, was in the parking lot about the same time you were talking to your friend. I believe he was spying on you and Victoria. Showing up once in a forest with binoculars is explainable, but to show up with them again in town, seems weird."

Chapter Eleven

The faint glow from the distant streetlight did little to illuminate the deserted parking lot at the wharf. Madison savored Micah's touch as his hand encircled hers. They drew nearer her car. She chuckled. "I suppose walking women to their vehicles may become a habit."

He offered a slight smile. "Right." He slipped his arm around her shoulders.

She turned to Micah when they arrived at her car. "Unless we see Ford again, I don't think we need to be too concerned." Madison leaned against the side of the vehicle. "I don't think I told you, but he checked into the inn on Sunday morning."

"Hey, you two. We keep running into each other."

Madison twirled around.

Micah reached for her hand and tugged her behind him.

A man wearing a floppy fishing hat and a fishing vest sporting fishing tackle lumbered toward them. "Thought I heard my name. You two doing okay?"

Micah fingered something at his waist. Was he carrying a gun? "Can I help you?"

Ford, the fishing hat drooping over his eyes, dangled

his arms at his side. "Just saying hello. I've been at the stream all day."

Madison started to speak, but Micah shook his head. "Where's your catch?"

Ford raised his hands wide. "I think the little lady is the best fisherman around us, Micah." He stepped forward.

Micah took a step back, gently moving Madison with him. "Someone saw you in town today, so I don't believe you were at the stream like you said."

"Now, who would go and say a thing like that," Ford balked and moved forward again.

"I warn you. I'm armed," Micah cautioned.

So he did carry a gun. Micah apparently wasn't taking any chances.

The man lifted both palms up as if to signal surrender. "You got me. I was only out there for a couple of hours. Before that I was working on a case, a leggy blonde. The one you were with today. I've been tasked with keeping an eye on her."

Micah relaxed, but Madison stayed on alert. "He could be lying," she whispered.

"She's a spoiled little rich girl, isn't she, Micah?"

Micah's grip on hers tightened once again. "Yes, she is."

Did Micah not like the man talking about Victoria the way he had? Could he actually be in love with his ex-patient and afraid to admit it.

"Daddy has her on a short leash. I'm following her to make sure she doesn't get into any trouble."

"Why would her father trust her into your watchful eye?" Micah challenged. "He's very protective of his little girl from what I recall."

"Yes. Yes. He is." The man reached under his vest.

Micah moved his hand to the gun.

Ford's gaze followed Micah's movement. He slipped his hand out. "I'm retrieving my business card." He held out his fingers, grasping a wallet with his thumb and forefinger.

When Micah relaxed, Ford did the same. He opened his wallet, pulled out a card, and stepped to give Micah the card.

"Madison, will you get it please," Micah said under his breath.

Madison reached for the card and stepped back just as quickly. "Ford Detective Agency," she read. "Micah, he's telling the truth."

Micah gave a curt nod. "Cranberry Cove is a small town. Strangers are noted. Strangers who look at residents through binoculars stand out even more, Mr. Ford. I'd think your experience would have taught you that."

Ford laughed with the same gravelly sound he'd given at the stream. "Warning heeded. Well, I'm starving." He nodded in Madison's direction. "I'll see you at the inn, little lady."

"Well, that explanation holds water." Madison breathed easy.

"Except for one thing," Micah turned to her.

She looked up into eyes filled with worry. "What?"

"If his assignment is Victoria, how'd he happen to know my name?"

Micah lingered with Madison beside her car, reluctant to let her go. She stood on tiptoes and kissed his cheek. "Thank you for dinner. No matter what happens, I feel safe when I'm with you."

Micah opened her driver's door. "I want to do everything I can to protect you." He ran his hand down her arm. He hadn't realized how much until he said the words. "We'll talk tomorrow."

"Oh, Dr. Collins. May I have a word please?"

Bates's voice was unmistakable. What now? He turned and did his best to layer politeness into his tone. "Hello, Bates. You enjoying your stay?"

Bates held out his hand for Micah to shake, but he smiled at Madison. "Hello, again."

Micah gritted his teeth. Bates had been the one to tell Madison about the past. If Bates wasn't here to make trouble, why had he circumvented Micah to approach someone who, at the time, Micah had barely known? But the man had asked for forgiveness.

Madison slipped her hand in Micah's and held tight. "Hello, to you as well."

He squeezed her fingers to offer assurance, he hoped.

Bates pumped Madison's hand up and down. "I'm so glad Dr. Collin's has made a friend here in Cranberry Cove. Especially after the tragedy he's suffered."

Madison nodded. "Yes, Micah's shared with me his previous circumstances, the ones you told me about." She took a few steps away from Bates.

Bates rubbed the back of his neck. "On my way from my walk to the bay, I saw the two of you chatting in the parking lot. Lovely town, this Cranberry Cove. First time I've really relaxed in months." He smiled. "But I digress. I wanted to reemphasize what I said before. I'm so sorry you suffered as you did. I sincerely want for us to be friends. If not friends, at least enjoy peace between us." He clapped Micah on the shoulder. "I mean that with all my heart. I'm glad your young lady is here, too."

Though Bates's expression was partially shrouded in the dark, for once, Micah believed the man. He stuck out his hand to shake his. "All right, Jax. I accept your offer of goodwill. No hard feelings between us."

Bates's smile stretched across his face. "Wonderful. I feel a hundred pounds lighter. Now, I know you two have better things than to stand around chatting with me." He nodded to Madison. "I hope to see you again before I leave."

Micah turned toward Madison. "I never expected those words from Bates. I believe he was sincere."

82

Chapter Twelve

The next afternoon, Micah secured the lock on the store's front door, blinked his tired eyes, and dialed Madison's number. Sleep had evaded him last night. The light of day still hadn't brought answers. Who was Ford actually spying on and for whom? Had Bates hired Ford to ferret out Micah's location? Could it have actually been Victoria, and that's how the man knew so much about her? Or was Ford telling the truth?

"Hey, Micah."

Madison's voice settled him. She understood his concerns, and he wanted her by his side. "Would you go with me to check out some houses? I can swing by your apartment in fifteen minutes."

"For The Caring Center?"

"Yeah. I saw one possibility on the edge of town near the city park."

"I'm all yours."

Would it be too much to hope her words referred to more than house hunting?

"Are you hungry?"

He chuckled. "Always."

"I made chicken sandwiches and fruit salad. Sound

good?"

His stomach growled. "My appetite says yes."

After he gassed up the car, he knocked at Madison's door. Calling her, stopping by her apartment, eating a meal together—all began to feel normal, natural. Was a possible relationship the direction he wanted his life to take? His heart voted yes, but his common sense warned *wait*.

Her smiling face at the door said he should take the advice of his heart. "I hope we don't run into Ford." She juggled a cooler in her arms.

"Let me take that." He set the container in the backseat of his car. "I thought of nothing else last night. Part of me says we need to stay cautious around him. Another part says he's telling the truth."

"Yeah, but it doesn't explain how he knew your name." Madison lowered her voice. "I've had other things on my mind, so I haven't made time to think it out."

"Are you okay?"

"I didn't mention this, but twice now, my ex contacted me. He texted me and then a few days later sent a huge bouquet of flowers to the inn. Today, he's tried to call me three times. I haven't answered."

"Do you suppose he's trying to reestablish a relationship with you?" Micah had to admit, the idea didn't set well with him. But then, how could he stand in the way if God was restoring a broken marriage.

Madison folded her arms over her chest. "If Josh thinks he can persuade me to go back to him—I'm sorry. It's not happening. I don't believe I could ever trust him again."

He opened the passenger door for her. "Let's take one

day at a time. But if anything happens, I'm here for you " He helped her in. "Let's go look at that house."

Fifteen minutes later and closer to the bay, he pulled off the road and onto a dirt driveway. A realtor's *for sale* sign sat in the front yard of the house. From the look and style—he estimated the age around fifty years.

Madison hopped out of his car and peeked into the front window of the small home sided with white hardie boards. "Looks empty."

Micah locked his car and peeked over Madison's shoulder through the window.

A fireplace filled one end of a large room. The walls needed fresh paint and the floors new tile. A hall on the other side led to rooms which might have been bedrooms. "This place is a distinct possibility." He strolled around to the backyard to catch a view of the other part of the house. He peeked in at the first window. A kitchen with out-of-date appliances would need upgrades.

A door slammed, and Micah strolled to the front again. "Madison, where did you go?" He glanced to his car. His vehicle sat empty.

A thick stand of trees grew around the property, casting shadows over the house and yard. He peered into the woods and returned to the rear of the house.

Micah stumbled over an exposed root and then regained his footing. Maybe Madison was inside the house and couldn't hear him. No problem.

Wandering around, a thought niggled at his brain. What if Madison's husband did come back into her life? Or what if he planned to cause trouble as she feared? He tapped his forehead. He didn't need to allow his imagination to explore ideas which might not be true.

He headed toward the other end of the house. A smaller room with an outside door appeared to have been added later. He opened the screen and turned the knob. The door pushed inward. "Hello. Anyone here?"

Silence.

Micah took a few steps into the area glancing from one side to the other. Madison's absence worried him. He needed to lay eyes on her, especially if Ford was someone after him.

The smaller room led to an adjoining space which must have served as a bedroom. He took the nearby hall and walked to the kitchen.

An exit to the outdoors sat on the backwall. He walked a few steps around the kitchen, and then the door creaked open. A chill worked its way down his spine. He shook his head. Why was he so jumpy?

Madison walked through clutching a couple of purple and yellow lilies. "I came inside and then heard footsteps in the backyard. I walked out to investigate and couldn't resist picking these flowers at the edge of the woods."

"It must've been about the time I left the backyard and entered on the other side of the house." Micah laughed. "I suppose we've been playing cat and mouse."

"Or mouse and cat." Madison giggled.

He resisted the urge to take her in his arms. "I was a bit concerned—you're here now." He caught his breath. "After last night and your worries about your ex-husband, for a moment, I imagined you could be in danger." He rubbed the back of his neck. "Stupid thought, I know."

"I think our imaginations could be working overtime."

"I hope that's all."

She looked around the room. "What do you think? I explored the whole house, and I think this could work. The small rooms might be used for private counseling. The larger areas for group sessions." She clasped her hands and smiled. "It's perfect, Micah."

Micah took another long breath. "Let's take a look at the for-sale sign. I'd like to get the realtor's information."

Micah circled around the side of the house and crossed the yard to the sign, Madison following. He snapped a picture of the sign with his phone number. Something white stuck on his windshield. "Look over there."

Madison frowned. "What's that? I don't remember seeing anything on your car when we arrived."

Micah neared the paper secured under the wipers. He pulled a torn paper cup from the window. *You could be in danger. Be careful* was scrawled with crude letters.

Madison peeked over his shoulder. "Who would scare us like this?" Madison's unsteady breath on his neck caused him to turn.

He looked around them at the peaceful area. Yes, who would want to break the tranquility here? "Bored teenagers could be up to no good." If only he felt as secure as his words sounded.

Madison followed Micah to his car.

He pulled out his cell phone, dialed the number on the for-sale sign, and waited. "Yes, ma'am. I'd like to confirm the list price of the house on Forest Drive." He leaned against his car and gave Madison a thumbs up. "Seems to be a fair price."

Her heart leapt. She and Micah had taken the first step in seeing his plan become reality—and so far, the project seemed plausible.

Micah shoved his cell phone into his pocket. "Come to my apartment, and we can enjoy that meal. I thought we could brainstorm possibilities to raise funds."

She climbed into Micah's car. The cooler in the backseat with the chicken salad and fruit bounced as they curved along the county road full of potholes and large rocks.

The memory of the note on Micah's car chilled her once more. Was it like Micah said? Teenagers acting out? An odd notion within told her there was more to the paper on his windshield than they thought. That paper meant that someone had followed them to the house. Were they still being stalked? People who had a strong faith in God would seek Him right about now. Wouldn't hurt to try.

Her faltering words emerged as a whisper. "God, please keep Micah from danger—and me, too." There. She'd spoken the prayer, but had Anyone heard?

After Micah pulled up to the curb, he hauled the cooler out of the car. His arms brushed hers as he took the handles and shuffled up his sidewalk. His touch ignited a flare of heat through her body.

She held the door as Micah set the cooler inside. His wide shoulders and slim hips captivated her.

In Micah's small kitchen, she opened the cooler and prepared two plates piled with the sandwiches and fruit. Would he say a prayer this time? She set the plates on the small table for two.

"I'd like to pray for a little more besides the meal." Micah grasped her hand. "Lord, thank You for Madison and this wonderful dinner. If You want The Caring Center to thrive, open the doors. If not, close the doors. Amen."

When she opened her eyes, Micah wore an easy smile. "Open doors?"

"Yes, if the Lord wants us to pursue this project, He'll provide opportunities to make this work. In my opinion, if we struggle every step of the way, it might be an indication that God has something else in mind."

She firmed her hands on the table. Micah had spoken to God as if He were real, an actual person. They'd communicated with the Deity she now believed to exist.

Micah patted her hand. "What are you thinking? You have the strangest look on your face."

She scooped a piece of fruit salad with her fork. "I'm amazed that you feel at home with God. You talk to Him anytime you want."

"That's what a relationship with Him is all about—one you can have, too."

Madison tensed and gripped her hands into balls. Did Micah actually know what he was talking about? "Let's talk about this another time."

"Sure. And later we can figure out details like funding, community support, possible remodeling." He scratched his head. "But no amount of planning will work unless we can purchase the house.

Chapter Thirteen

Bates sipped his coffee and peered out the front of the cottage at the bay. He gave himself a mental pat on the back. Coming to Cranberry Cove had been a wise move. And renting the seaside cabin provided more room to roam.

He returned to the small kitchen and poured another cup of coffee. No place could compete with the view. If he could convince his son, Liam, to make a visit, he had an extra bedroom in the rental.

He set down his cup when his phone rang. Victoria's number. "Hello. How are things at the inn?"

"I need to talk to you—right away." The agitation in her voice said she wasn't happy about something.

"Fine, but I suggest you come to my cabin instead of meeting at the inn."

"Whatever. Give me the address. I can be there in fifteen."

Bates picked up his t-shirt from yesterday and a couple pairs of shoes. Better hit the laundry soon.

Twenty minutes later, he answered the tap on his door.

Victoria walked into the cabin like royalty and

glanced around. "So, how do you like the cabin?"

Bates swung around to face her. "This place suits my tastes. If a bunch of fishermen can stay here, it's okay for me."

She walked to the couch and plopped down. "To each his own."

He edged down on the other end. "Are you enjoying your time away from Sacramento?"

She crossed one leg over the other. "When we ran into each other in Sacramento, you indicated that there could be hope for me and Micah. I don't think that's true."

He scooted a few inches closer. "You must remember Micah suffered as I did—from the loss of a wife."

She folded her arms over her chest and stared at him.

"He needs time. Micah's healing from a traumatic life situation. Be patient."

"But what if you're wrong, and he doesn't have feelings for me. I seriously don't like rejection, and I hate it when I can't have what I want. I'd been through counseling because of the cancer, and I'd gotten past wanting Micah. You opened that door for me again."

Bates stood and paced the floor. Everything was always someone else's fault with her kind. Yes, he'd hinted strongly to get her here, but the move was on her, not on him. "You not only want things, you want them when you want them. Have you ever considered that winning Micah might take some time? He's been captivated by another woman. He hasn't thought much of you with her in his life. You have to remind him of what he thought of you in Sacramento. She needs to be taken out of the picture."

Victoria shook her head. "If he ever had feelings for me, he has a strange way of showing it."

Bates blew out a silent breath of frustration. "Look, as one who has faced the loss of a wife, I can honestly say that if I was given a choice between two beautiful women, I'd have a hard time reaching out and committing totally to either of them. Mary is always there. However, I'd enjoy their company whenever I could without making a commitment. Your choice is to hang in the background and wait for him to be ready for that commitment to you or step up your game. You'll lose him if you don't do the latter

She uncrossed her legs. "When you put it like that … "

Bates flopped down on the couch again. "Listen to the words of experience dear. Men are pathetic at best. Add grief to our plates and we're just plain idiots."

Madison glanced at the clipboard with the list of rooms to prepare. She retrieved her cleaning caddy from the laundry room and stepped into the kitchen.

"Hey, Madison." Ashton balanced her toddler on her hip and scribbled some notes on the menu planner with her other hand. "How's your new hobby going? I haven't seen you in the studio for a couple of days."

Warmth circled her insides as she remembered what had occupied her time. "Hanging out with Micah. He wants to start a ministry for cancer victims."

Ashton switched her toddler to her other hip. "I wonder why he's interested in that."

"Er—" What could she say without going into detail about his life in Sacramento? "He's a strong Christian, and I believe he has a compassionate heart." There. She'd told Ashton the truth—only a small part. "We've got to work on raising funds before anything else."

"James and I would be happy to contribute through the inn."

"You may be our first." Madison smiled. "I'll let Micah know." She turned to head upstairs.

Ashton lifted her finger. "Oh, Victoria Brackenridge, the woman who checked in a few days ago, wanted extra pillows."

"No problem. I'll leave some in her room."

Ashton's baby squirmed and protested his position on her hip with a squeal. "Okay, honey. Gotta get you home for your nap."

"I have to start cleaning rooms, too. Thanks for your offer to support Micah's project." She blew a kiss to Ashton and headed up the stairs.

In the linen closet, Madison pulled out two down-filled pillows, walked to room ten, and tapped on the door.

No answer.

"Housekeeping. I have your pillows."

Still no answer. Miss Brackenridge was obviously not there. She unlocked the door with her master key. Madison set the two pillows on the bed she'd made up earlier and turned to leave.

A pair of stilettos on the floor caught her eyes. She stepped nearer. Gucci. A pink leather Chanel purse sat on the dresser. Madison puckered her lips in a silent whistle. This woman had expensive taste in clothes. Well, what did she expect after seeing the kind of car she drove—a Porsche?

Madison stepped out of the room and locked the door

again. Micah said the gorgeous, wealthy blond was a patient. Did Madison actually believe he'd only had a patient-doctor relationship with her? Surely, he wouldn't have consoled himself with her company after his wife's death.

That evening in the studio, Madison held the glass suncatcher she'd created up to the light and smiled. She'd created her first stained-glass project, a sunflower. Finding the crystal beads at Goodwill proved to be a blessing. The pale yellows completed the lovely daisy design.

For a beginner, she was pleased with her piece. Of course, she had her teacher to thank. Though the lessons began to get expensive, she deemed the pleasure of the craft worth the money.

Micah's large brown eyes bore into her memory. She had a multitude of questions for him that she hadn't had a chance to ask. The meaning of the words on her keychain. The apparent change in Tony's life. Maybe Micah could meet her for a cup of coffee tomorrow morning.

She turned her suncatcher over in her hand and smiled. Time for her to go home for the night.

She lifted her purse from her chair and spun toward the door, a lilt in her step.

Movement outside her side window brought her to a stop. She blinked.

Someone moved away from the glass, ducking down as if not wanting to be caught.

Madison rushed to turn off the overhead lights. Darkness settled over the studio. She crept to the window and peered out.

In the distance, a woman raced across the yard. She wore a skirt and her head was covered with some type of cloth. Her peeping Tomalina disappeared around the side of the inn.

She released the breath she'd held, yet her feet were frozen to the floor. Had they been spying on her, or had one of the inn's patrons been out for a walk, saw the light, and looked in out of curiosity? Even with such an innocent scenario, Madison imagined getting caught in the act would be embarrassing and cause the person to leave quickly before being approached.

She moved to the door and stopped after opening it as one particular female patron came to mind. Why spy on her?

If it had been Victoria, there could have been more to the incident than curiosity. The woman had, after all, followed Micah to Cranberry Cove from Sacramento.

Madison locked the studio door and walked to her car. If her suspicions were correct, Madison would hear from Victoria again.

Chapter Fourteen

Micah gripped the phone and pumped his fist. *Thank You, Lord.* "That's good news, Pastor Ethridge. I understand your congregation doesn't have assets to contribute, but I appreciate you reaching out to reputable ministries willing to help fund The Caring Center."

"I spoke with Mr. Russell who runs a ministry out of Tacoma," Pastor's deep voice rumbled in Micah's ear. "He said he was interested but had to talk to his board."

"Thank you, sir. Hope to see you soon." He clicked disconnect and rose from his desk.

Shuffling sounded and then a hard thud and the falling of items off a shelf rent the silence out front.

He bolted through the office door.

Near the entrance of the store, a customer, her graying hair in a bun, held her hand to her mouth and looked toward the floor. "Oh, no."

Someone must've tripped and fallen. Karina generally checked the floor for stray items, so he couldn't imagine … He navigated between shelves to the front and sipped in a quick breath.

Karina lay on the floor, one hand on her forehead. She groaned.

Micah kneeled beside her. "Karina, what happened?" He rolled up a couple of beach towels to elevate her legs.

"What's wrong with her?" The gray-haired woman huddled next to another lady dressed in a purple shirt, both women staring at his assistant manager.

He felt Karina's forehead. Cool and moist. "She must've lost consciousness for a moment."

The woman in the purple shirt retrieved her cell phone. "Do you want me to call 9-1-1?"

"No. Don't call." Karina moaned. "I'll be fine."

Micah held up his palm to the purple shirt lady. Bending down, he moved the items Karina's fall had pushed to the floor. "Let me take a look at her. I … er … have training in first aid." He felt for Karina's pulse. Maybe she was diabetic or had low blood pressure.

Karina attempted to rise. "I got lightheaded and lost my balance."

Micah supported her back, helping her to sit up. "Don't try to stand." He held her hand. "Do you have a headache or feel nauseous?"

"Yes." Karina rubbed her forehead.

"What about vision changes or ringing in your ears? Any history of heart trouble?"

"No, none of that."

Something caused the loss of consciousness. "Are you taking medications which would trigger dizziness?"

"Yes." She paused as she glanced at him. "Micah, can we talk … in private."

Micah glanced at the two customers watching them. "Ladies, thank you for your concern. Let's give Karina some space."

"Of course." The gray-haired woman glanced at Micah. "You seemed so confident. You must be well trained in first aid. Are you a nurse?"

Not a nurse but a doctor. "No, ma'am. I'm sorry I can't help you now. Please come back later today or tomorrow …"

"Of course. I understand. Karina, I hope you feel better soon." Gray-haired lady left with purple shirt following.

Micah studied Karina's skin tone. Some of the color had returned. "Are you able to stand?"

She nodded and gripped his arm.

Micah helped her to her feet and to the storage area in back. "Sit down." He assisted her into a nearby chair.

"I'm so sorry, Micah. I didn't mean to cause a problem."

"Don't think anything about it." He felt for her pulse again. "You said you wanted to talk."

She wiped at the moisture on her cheek. "There's something I need to tell you. I've put it off because I'm afraid I'll lose my job."

He slipped into a chair next to hers. "You're a competent employee. I can see no reason why that would happen." Even pregnancy wouldn't be a problem. Blake would likely be fine with granting an employee maternity leave.

She blinked back another tear. "A few months before I began my job, I was diagnosed with cervical cancer. My doctor performed a hysterectomy, and I started chemotherapy. I will lose my hair soon." She patted her eyes with a tissue. "I knew I should've told Blake." She swallowed a sob. "But I needed this job because my insurance doesn't cover all the expenses."

"Look, I believe Blake will understand." He patted her hand.

"My doctor said my cancer is at stage one. I'm grateful for that."

"Statistically speaking, patients in stage one have a ninety-two percent chance of survival." He smiled. "You'll beat this." He had to offer hope.

"I want to be around for my little boy, Juan."

"I'll be happy to help in any way I can."

She sniffed. "Traditionally, my family has many children. My mother-in-law wanted more than one grandchild. It's not going to happen now." She hid her face in her hands, and her shoulders shook.

He stared at the woman, and his heart raced. Karina's loss was more than cancer. She'd lost the ability to naturally birth a large family. In her anxiety and grief, she would be a perfect candidate for The Caring Center. "Listen to me. A center is opening soon that will assist cancer patients and their families. Though the service isn't available now, we're working hard to get it open." God willing.

Her sobs diminished. "There's something about you— " She shook her head. "I don't know."

Micah scrubbed a hand over his chin. Someday soon, he could tell her about his previous career. In the meantime, he prayed he could comfort her.

"Thank you for helping me off the floor."

"You're welcome. Losing consciousness is a possible side effect of your cancer diagnosis and the treatment you're undergoing. If the issue continues, I recommend you speak to your doctor."

"This is the first time I've passed out."

"Sit here for a while. Is there someone you'd like me to call?"

"No. I want to go back to work in a few minutes."

"Let's see how you feel." He handed her a bottle of water from the minifridge. "I better keep an eye on the front." Micah walked to the floor again. His phone rang, and Madison's name appeared on the screen.

"Micah, can you meet with me?"

"Do you want to go to dinner in Oceanview? We could take a walk on the beach and talk?" he suggested.

"How could I say no to a sunset stroll by the ocean?" What sounded like anxiety in her voice fled, replaced by her laughter.

"Great. I'll pick you up in an hour."

"Can't wait."

And neither could he.

Madison sank her toes into the grains of soft sand tickling the bottoms of her feet. White clouds dotted the sky near the ocean's surface. The sun dipped lower on the horizon, painting the water and beach with golds and oranges. Though the strange woman's appearance hung over her like a puzzle needing a solution, strolling on the water's edge with Micah soothed her fears. Who would believe she'd have a relationship with another man? But now a life with Micah filled her thoughts. "My grilled tuna steak with peach salsa was delicious."

"Mine, too." He clasped her hand. "Walking on the beach at sunset is fun when I'm with you."

She savored his large, warm hand holding hers. The same hand that performed intricate surgeries to save women's lives. The thought intrigued her. "I feel the same."

"You mentioned you wanted to tell me something about last night?"

A saltwater breeze lifted a strand of her hair. "The sound of the waves and the sunset. I hate to ruin our evening." The wind caught the edge of her shirt, and she tugged it down. "Last night at the studio when I put my equipment away, someone was looking through the window—a woman. She ran around the side of the inn." She squeezed his hand.

"Could you identify her?" he asked.

"Her head was covered, but that's not unusual. Some women do put a scarf around them at night to keep the humidity from doing crazy things to their hair."

"But you think the stranger could be Victoria?" He stopped and faced her.

"I thought so."

He rubbed his forehead. "I doubt Victoria would want to cause you any harm. She's a bit high strung and spoiled, prone to a temper tantrum, but I don't think she meant to stress you out."

Madison nodded. "I thought the same thing, but may I ask a personal question?"

"Sure. I have nothing to hide from you."

She cleared her throat. Though none of her business, she needed to confirm her theory. "Could Victoria be in love with you?"

He shrugged. " I think she's attracted to me because I was there for her as her doctor through a scary time in her life. I cautioned her family when they pampered her—that they were hurting more than helping. They spoiled her, gave her whatever she wanted. Even if she thinks herself in love with me, what she could be feeling is far from love. Why do you ask?"

"Could she see me as competition?" Madison's face burned. "Not that we uh … Since we're together a lot, things might look romantic to her."

He chuckled. "I never thought about that."

She picked up a shell and brushed off the sand. "In a completely unrelated question, do you know Tony, the chef at the inn?"

"No. The only chef I met was Juliette when Ryder brought her to the store." He smiled. "He used to talk about her all the time."

"There's no doubt they loved each other." Madison sighed. She should know. She'd pursued Ryder, and he'd rejected her.

Micah raised his eyebrows. "Why did you ask about Tony?"

"I can't figure him out. He stole from Ashton and compromised Juliette's job. Then Ashton fired him. Now he's working at the inn again and claims God changed his life."

Micah held her hand to his chest. "With God all things are possible. If Tony asked Jesus, God's son, to forgive him of what he did and accepted the Savor's sacrifice on the cross, then he has a new nature. He has a new way of thinking and behaving."

"You're telling me that Tony can't steal anymore?"

"No. He could because he still has free will, but now his desires and goals are different. It's like me. I could misrepresent the invoices and bank deposits at the store for my own gain, but I would never steal from Blake because I know it's wrong." He looked deeper into her eyes. "I would never bring harm to you, either."

"Oh?" Her heart pattered in her chest.

"People change after they give their lives to the Lord.

There are exceptions, I'm afraid."

"Because of free will."

"Yes."

The sun sank under the horizon propelling shafts of gold light in its wake. "You've given me a lot to think about."

Micah released her hand and took a few steps along the beach. "No man could change another person. Tony is a new creature with a new heart."

Madison glanced toward the sky as a lone star became visible. "Do you remember the day we went to the lake, and we talked about how nature reflected God?"

"Yes, Romans 1:19."

She pointed to the sky. "See that star. One of billions. There's another reason to be certain about God. To think the universe came into existence of its own accord is ludicrous."

Micah lifted his straight, well-shaped nose and sniffed. "Nothing like the aroma of salt air and seaweed. All of nature indicates a Supreme Being Who loves us."

Madison caught his hand in hers. "I'm ready to know more about your God."

Chapter Fifteen

Madison walked in through the inn's side door. She waved at Tony as he pulled a large tray of cinnamon rolls from the oven ready to be slathered with the gooey icing. Her tennis shoes tapped the hardwood floor in the main hall as she headed toward Ashton's office.

Memories of last night on the beach with Micah—the sand, saltwater air, and sky, lingered in her thoughts, tingling her insides. Micah's words describing a changed life made sense, drew her in, inspired her to know more of his faith. She tapped on Ashton's office door and entered.

"Good morning." Ashton perused her computer screen. "I'm looking for a new plumber. Our usual man is selling his company, and the sink in room five is leaking."

"Hmm. Room five?"

"Yes. A Mr. Ford from Sacramento, California."

She hadn't seen Mr. Ford since running into him in the parking lot, but apparently, he was still around. "Will do." Madison picked up the clipboard with the daily room assignments and marked room five.

A grin filled Ashton's face. "How's it going with you

and Micah?"

"Going? There's nothing going — "

"Madison Mitchell, we've been friends for years. I see that glimmer in your eyes. You like him, don't you?"

Madison hiked her hand on her waist. "You don't know what you're talking about." She couldn't disguise her smile. "Okay, maybe a little."

"Now, Madison. I need the truth."

"All right. Maybe a lot."

"Uh huh." Ashton folded her arms over her chest. "Let's hear the rest."

Madison slipped into the chair opposite her boss. "There's nothing to tell. I've enjoyed working with him setting up a ministry for cancer patients and their families. And … " Memories of last night's walk on the beach delighted her senses.

"And what?"

"I like being with him. We've talked about God and how He created all things. Micah spoke about the way peoples' lives change—how they receive a new nature when they ask Jesus to forgive them. Take Tony, for example."

Ashton reached across her desk and squeezed Madison's hand. "Micah is correct. Both James and I found the peace and joy a new life can bring."

The old doubts still weighed on Madison's mind. She rose and gripped the clipboard. "I need to get to work."

"I love you, my friend." Ashton smiled and returned to her computer.

Madison closed the door as she retraced her steps to the kitchen. She picked up her supply caddy. Ashton, James, Micah, and even Tony possessed something special. She couldn't deny it. But she sensed she needed to wait.

After cleaning the downstairs rooms, she climbed the majestic staircase, stopping on the way to admire Gina's beautiful stained-glass window.

Sometime later, she mopped her damp forehead. Finally, all the second story rooms were clean except Mr. Ford's room. She picked up a set of fresh sheets from the upstairs linen closet and tapped at the door. No answer. "Housekeeping." Still no sound. She unlocked the door with her master key and walked in with her cleaning bucket. After she'd cleaned the bathroom and changed the sheets, she turned to dust the dresser top.

A picture on the dresser caught her eye. She gasped and picked it up, turning it over in her hand. The picture was of Micah, a snapshot taken when he apparently hadn't been aware of it, but what chilled her were the pinprick holes pushed into Micah's face. She pulled her phone from her pocket and took a shot of it. Why would Mr. Ford have a picture of Micah let alone one that was mutilated?

A footfall on the landing outside caught Madison's attention. She tossed the photo on the dresser and shoved her phone back into her pocket.

The doorknob turned, and Madison picked up her bucket of cleaning supplies.

Mr. Ford opened the door and stilled. Then he smiled. "Little lady." He nodded. "I can see I forgot to leave the sign on my door letting you know I wouldn't need the room cleaned."

"It's okay. I did a light cleaning." She motioned around pointing to the pile of dirty sheets and towels she'd left by the door to retrieve when she finished her job. "Made the bed, cleaned the bathroom." Leaving out the dusting was a necessary misdirection. "I've just finished." She stepped around him. "Have a wonderful afternoon."

Her skin crawled as she closed his door.

She took the sheets and towels to the laundry and added them with the others, readying them to wash. Her phone rang, and she answered. "Hey," Micah said. "Could you meet me at the house we're looking to purchase around three this afternoon? The head of Rejoice in Hope Cancer Ministries out of Tacoma would like to see the facility but wants to hear more about our vision first. They're very interested in funding part of our project. Our real-estate agent will meet us at the property."

Her heart pounded. "I'll be sure to finish up here and be on my way."

After Pastor Ethridge left, Micah shook hands with Mr. Russell and watched him pull away from the curb. The Caring Center of Cranberry Cove, God willing, would be theirs as soon as they raised the rest of the money.

He joined Madison as they waved good-bye to the agent, and then he gave Madison a high five.

She threw her arms around him, hugged him tight, and took a couple of steps back. "I can't believe Mr. Russell's ministry is willing to fund half the cost of the house."

"Yes, thanks to Pastor Ethridge's help."

Madison moved away, but the fresh scent of lavender

and vanilla lingered, accelerating his pulse.

She leaned against the for-sale sign. "You did a great job of presenting our goals to Mr. Russell."

"Thank you, but I can't claim credit. We're doing the Lord's business." He brushed a strand of hair off his forehead.

"If we want the house, we need to submit an offer as soon as possible. The realtor did hint that there are other buyers who're interested."

"We'll bid more than the listing price which should give us an advantage." Micah couldn't take his eyes off Madison in her well-fitting jeans and turquoise top that matched her eyes. He shook his head. He had to concentrate on the ministry. "I'm expecting a text from Mr. Russell about sending the funds. He said the money would likely be available toward the first part of next week."

Madison gazed at the house. "I bet in six months' time the center will buzz with activity."

"I have a potential candidate now. Of course, the names of attendees will be confidential, but I can tell you my assistant manager has expressed an interest." He stepped closer to Madison and ran his hands down her shoulders. They felt stiff, and she twisted a long strand of light brown hair. "Is there something wrong?"

She pulled her cell phone from her pocket. "I cleaned the rooms at the inn this morning. I saw a picture on the dresser in room five." She scrolled a few times and then held the screen toward him. "It's a picture of you."

He held the phone to closer look at the image. "I don't remember the shot, but it looks like I'm outside my practice in Sacramento." He continued to stare at the picture.

"I'm not sure if you can see them, but your face is marked with pinpricks, tiny holes as if someone pushed pins into the photograph."

"What does it mean?"

"Can you tell me the name of the guest staying in the room?"

"Yes. That's what has me very frightened, Micah. The guest is Mr. Ford from Sacramento."

Micah's chest tightened. "If he's keeping an eye on Victoria, why would he do something like that to a photo of me?"

Madison gripped his hand. "He lied to us."

The pressure of her fingers on his relieved some of his angst. "I don't know. If I'm his focus, how did he know so much about Victoria? Something isn't right here, it's as if we're missing a piece of the puzzle."

And that puzzle was beginning to take on the form of a nightmare.

Chapter Sixteen

The next morning, Micah unlocked the heavy glass door to Sloan's Fishing Supplies. Saturday was a busy day so he might as well get started early.

Blake hadn't come in lately. From the conversation he had with him a few weeks ago at church, Blake spent much of his time at the VA center. His boss trusted Micah to run the store efficiently. He couldn't disappoint his Christian brother who offered a job when Micah needed one.

Micah switched on the lights and glanced around at the shelves. Karina always left the store straightened and clean. He'd prayed for her this morning, and God had heard, no doubt.

When his phone buzzed, he fished in his pocket. Pastor Ethridge. "Good morning, sir."

"Micah. So glad I caught you. I got some good news last night. I heard from Be Not Afraid Ministry out of Spokane. The board members have been looking for a Christian organization that ministers to cancer patients and their families. Based upon my recommendation, they'd like to fund the other half of the cost on the house you want to purchase."

"Pastor, that's amazing." Micah resisted the urge to

shout halleluiah. "I can't thank you enough for your help."

"You will someday when I see cancer victims and their families finding comfort, fellowship, and direction."

Micah raked his hand through his hair, tamping down the emotion rising in his throat. "Looks like The Caring Center will be up and running before we know it." He disconnected and called Madison.

"I was thinking about you. I gotta show off my first stained-glass creation. A sunflower. You want to meet me at the studio later this afternoon?"

"Yes, definitely, but first I want to ask you—would you go with me to the realty office?"

"Sure. Ashton doesn't need me today. What's up?"

"Are you sitting down? We got the rest of the funding for The Caring Center."

"Yahoo!" she squealed.

Micah moved the phone away from his ear and laughed.

"That's fantastic. Remember when you told me about open and closed doors? I think we heard one squeak open."

"Good reminder. I'd forgotten what I said." He smiled knowing Madison had listened that day. "I'd like to make an offer on the house today. I talked to Janette at the realty office yesterday, and she said she could write a contract as soon as I was ready. I told her I was waiting for the capital, but with the funds due in a couple of days, I can front the escrow deposit."

The door jingled and Karina walked in.

My assistant manager is here. "Can you meet me in a half hour?"

"You got it."

The sign with Town and Country Realty extended from the steepled roof of the red brick building with the wide glass windows. Madison's beam boosted Micah's joy as he held the white wooden door for her.

A middle-aged woman looked up from a desk at the entrance and smiled.

Micah stepped toward her. "We'd like to see Janette, please. I spoke with her yesterday, but I don't have an appointment."

"No problem." The receptionist dialed an in-house phone and glanced up. "She's in her office down the hall."

Janette waited at the open door, a smile missing from her usual happy expression. "Come in, please." She motioned to the chairs in front of her desk.

Micah scooted into the chair next to Madison and peered at her with a silent question—*what's going on?*

The agent sank into her office chair, stacked some papers into a neat pile, and glanced up. "Only moments ago, I'd planned to call you, Micah, but another agent came in the office for a file he needed." She folded her hands on her desk. "Yesterday evening, the owner of the property you're interested in took the listing off the market. I'm so sorry."

Micah heart dropped to his stomach. "I ... off the market? I don't know what to say. I was so sure ... "

Madison frowned and gripped his arm.

"Did he say why?" Micah held his hand up. "No, I'm

sorry. That's none of my business."

"It's all right. His listing agent said he learned his oldest daughter was returning to the area, and he needs the house for her family." She perused her computer screen. "There's nothing available right now in that price range, but I'll certainly be watching the market."

Micah stood and held his hand to shake hers. "Thank you, Janette. You've been so helpful. Please let us know." He swallowed the disappointment that threatened to emerge.

Madison shook her hand. "Yes, we appreciate your help." She turned to Micah and slipped her arm into his.

Outside of the building, Micah trudged down the sidewalk, Madison's arm still gripping his.

"I'm confused, Micah. I thought we had an open door."

Micah rubbed his hand over his chin. "The Bible tells us God's ways are not our ways. He has His reasons. Perhaps there's a better property out there He wants us to have."

"So, we wait?"

"That's about it."

Madison pointed toward the street. "I feel like walking. The city park's over there."

He nodded, and they crossed the road.

The sun shone in the blue sky, sending sparkles of light reflecting from the Douglas fir and the evergreen bushes. Yet the brilliance didn't seem to lift his gloom. He kicked at a discarded Styrofoam cup. He wasn't good at dealing with disappointment.

Hand in hand, they wandered along the path and stopped at a park bench. Beyond the seat, huckleberry bushes and maple vines bordered a circular, azure lake.

"Let's sit a moment," Micah said.

Madison settled on the bench and scooted closer to him. "We'll find another house. You'll realize your dream someday."

"I can't understand why God provided all of the funds right when the house went off the market."

A gray squirrel swished his tail and scurried up the trunk of a nearby tree. God's creature didn't worry about where they'd live or what they'd eat. God took care of them. He'd provide for his and Madison's needs, as well.

"I don't know much about God, but I can see something different in the people who believe in Him."

Micah couldn't help but smile. "Who do you mean?"

"Ryder, Tony, Ashton, and James … you. I see a greater purpose in your lives—peace. I don't know, Micah. It's hard to describe. Perhaps hope is the word."

Micah faced her and held her hand. "I've found meaning. I no longer merely trudge through life without purpose. Or try to make more money than my neighbors, or possess more things. Or climb the corporate ladder. Life may not go the way I'd like sometimes, but my time on earth makes sense."

"Makes sense?"

"Yes, I know who I am and why I'm here—to serve my Creator and enjoy His presence."

Madison rested her shoulders against the bench and exhaled a deep breath. "I have a lot to learn about your God."

"He's willing to come into your life," Micah whispered. Though this wasn't the right time, he leaned closer, longing to find out how Madison's full pink lips felt on his.

As if offering permission, she ran her fingers down

his cheek.

With only an inch separating them, his phone buzzed, sounding louder than usual. He moved from Madison and retrieved his cell from his pocket. "Bad timing," he muttered. "Hello."

"Blake here. I wanted to give you the good news, and let you know I may not be in the store for another week."

Micah blinked. "What's up, buddy?"

"Next time I see you, I have a cigar for you. I'm a father. Gracie had her baby early this morning. We have a little girl."

"Congratulations. And don't worry about the store." He still wanted to tell Blake about Karina but—another time.

"If you ever get married, I'm telling you—there's nothing like fatherhood. Our little girl—she's so tiny. I can't believe she's mine and Gracie's."

No need to tell Blake he had been married once. Micah chuckled. "Okay, okay, man. I'll remember what you said." He hung up and slipped his phone in his pocket. How many times had he seen the look of joy on parents' faces when their baby arrived?

He glanced at the woman beside him with firm, flawless skin and strands of long hair gracing her shoulders. If they had a child someday, would Madison make a good parent? Would he? First, he and Madison needed the same understanding of God. "That was Blake. Gracie had her baby."

"Oh, that's so exciting. Mrs. Mayberry is a grandmother." She studied his face. "Micah, don't worry about The Caring Center. We'll find another place." She patted his hand. "When you get off work, stop by my studio, and I'll show you my first stained-glass creation."

He smiled. "I'd love to." But would her prediction they'd find another place come to pass? Only God knew.

"Take a long lunch, Karina." In the back of the store, Micah waved his fingers to shoo his employee away. "You worked all morning while I was out."

"I won't argue with that." She smiled and grabbed her purse. Her shorter, dark brown wig helped to cover her hair loss.

"Hey, Karina. I wanted to tell you how pleased I am with your work performance. Chemotherapy isn't getting you down." He patted her back. "You're doing a great job."

"Thanks, Micah." The door dinged as she walked out the door.

Micah straightened some fishing vests on the sale table and headed toward the front. He waited at the cash register for a customer who approached with fishing lures and two jars of salmon eggs in his hands. "Yes, sir."

The man placed the items on the counter and pulled out his credit card.

A ding alerted him another customer had entered the store.

Micah placed the man's items in a bag and handed him the receipt. "Come back to see us again."

"Well, hello, Dr. Collins," Bates's greeting and the pronunciation of Micah's title and last name seemed to bely his proclaimed forgiveness.

Micah's instincts warned him to remain alert. "Mr. Bates, what can I do for you?"

Bates glanced around the store and widened his eyes. "Your store is well maintained, I see. Your expert touch is evident in every shelf and rack. Expertly organized like your medical practice."

The store was empty. Time had come to have a heart-to-heart with the man. "Just now, when you addressed me, I noted some disdain in your voice. Are you sure you've moved on from Mary's death?"

Bates winched and his shoulders slumped. "I apologize, Micah. I suppose I have my moments of weakness. Forgiveness is something we practice, isn't it? That is, until we get it right. I do mean every word I said. I always did admire your skills as a doctor. Mary's death disheartened me for a while. As if my spirit simply died." He looked toward the ceiling and then made eye contract. "But I've changed." He leaned toward Micah, and his eyes took on a hint of glee. "It's God, you know. He changes a person."

Micah gulped. Though a few doubts still remained, how could he challenge his sincerity about the Lord? "I'm glad to hear it. I wish you the best. Now, how can I help you?"

Bates smiled. "I broke my rod yesterday. I'd like to purchase a new one—a good one. The price isn't a concern. I can't say enough good things about this little resort town hidden down here in southern Washington."

Micah stepped away from the counter. "We keep our best models—or our most expensive ones—in the back of the store." He led Bates to the display.

"If you can get off one of these days, we could hit the streams together."

"Yeah … well, I give fishing instructions to customers who sign up. Not sure when I can fit in a fishing trip for myself." Micah would gladly see the tension between them end, but he wasn't about to go fishing with the guy.

Bates paused at the display. He seemed to be milling over something in his mind. "If I signed up for a lesson, that would get you out there with me, wouldn't it?"

Micah hesitated.

Bates shook his head. "I mean, it would allow you to join me. I wouldn't mind if you brought your friend along."

The fishing lessons were given as a part of the cost for a new rod and reel if a person chose to take advantage. Without good enough reason, Micah couldn't refuse a customer.

Still, he prayed Bates would forget about the perk.

Chapter Seventeen

Madison relaxed in the inn's elegant living room listening to Ashton's description of how her toddler was getting into everything now that he was walking. "You're a wonderful mother, Ashton. I admire your patience."

"I'm sure one day you'll—"

Madison bounded up. "Gotta go. Micah's stopping by the studio to see my suncatcher." Having a child seemed unlikely, and she didn't want to talk about it. She couldn't fall into envying her best friend's life.

"All right, sweetie. Have fun with your gorgeous boyfriend."

"Ashton Atwood. We haven't officially referred to each other as girlfriend and boyfriend." Maybe they never would. She waved as she walked down the hall, strolled through the kitchen, and out the back door to the deck.

Again, she remembered Micah's lips only inches from hers earlier today. If his phone hadn't rung, she would've allowed him to kiss her. Though she'd sworn she'd never become involved with another guy, she had to acknowledge the truth. Her feelings for Micah were unlike any she'd ever known. Though she wasn't ready to admit the information to Ashton quite yet.

She glanced toward the inn's side parking lot.

Micah pulled up next to her car and got out.

Madison continued down the path to the studio. A tingle tickled her stomach. What would he say about her stained-glass?

She retrieved her keychain from her purse and gripped the nob. Before she could place the key in the lock, the door swung open. She glanced over her shoulder at Micah. "That's odd. I could've sworn I locked this door when I left yesterday."

Micah frowned and slipped in front of her. "Stay here for a second." He entered.

Madison stayed back until he returned. "No one's here. Let's look around. See if anything is missing." He examined the new cabinet where she stored some of her supplies.

Madison followed him in and crept closer to her workbench where she'd left her stained-glass piece.

The busted frame was on the floor, and a pile of tiny shards of glass, mostly yellow in color, lay on one side of her workspace. She bent down and put her hand to her chest. "I worked so hard on this." Her very first work of art, destroyed.

"Could it have fallen off the table?" Micah stooped beside her.

She shook her head. "I was very careful. This is my first piece of art, created by my own hands. I've invested time and effort into it. I would never have been that careless. Who would do this? And how did they get in?"

"Could you have accidentally not shut the door? Maybe Ashton came in looking for something, and she left it ajar. A neighborhood cat might have gotten in. They're famous for knocking things off tables."

"Ashton recognizes this as my space now. Even if she has a second key, she would have asked or told me she needed to get inside, and I know that I shut and locked the door. After the woman..." Her heart and her words stopped at the same time. "You said she has a temper..."

"Victoria?"

"Yes, Victoria." Madison pushed to her feet. "She has to be the one who was outside my window the other day."

"Let's not jump to conclusions before we check with Ashton to see if anyone could have gotten a second key." He moved to the door and opened it, examining the keyhole and the frame. "I don't see any forced entry."

"And it's just a silly stain-glass." She crossed her arms. "Why get worked up?"

Micah rushed back to her. "That's not what I'm saying." He touched her face with his warm hand. "The piece means a lot to me because I know how much making it meant to you, but Victoria deserves the benefit of the doubt until we have the evidence to confront her. So far, if it was her outside the other night, it could have been an innocent look inside and getting caught caused embarrassment."

Madison sighed. "I'm so sorry. Talk about a temper tantrum." She tried to shrug off the vandalism, but disappointment weighed her down. "I'll check with Ashton about a second key." She swiped a tear from her cheek. Her hard work—destroyed. She gave a look around. "Why do you suppose whoever was in here didn't do more damage?"

Micah shook his head. "I'm not sure. Perhaps they thought it more vindictive to ruin your project. Perhaps to frighten you. Make you believe that if they could break in once, they could do it again." He drew her close and lingered, his arms tightly around her. "I don't mean to upset you." He took a few steps back and frowned. "I'm beginning to wonder if we're not both the target of someone or two different people."

Madison shivered. "Josh is the only other suspect I have, but I'm not sure why, and he's been quiet lately."

"Sometimes it's the silence that can be most worrying."

After Madison agreed to attend church with Micah and afterward having a picnic lunch, he left. Madison secured the studio door and headed toward the kitchen entrance. Inside the inn, Ashton spoke with Mrs. Mayberry and glanced up. "The guests are in for a treat tonight. Tony's off, but Mrs. Mayberry's trying her hand at German cuisine."

Madison inhaled the enticing aroma of schnitzel, hissing and popping in hot oil, as well as whiffs of lemon, olive oil, and asparagus. "You're making me hungry. What's for dessert?"

Mrs. Mayberry smiled. "Black forest cake, of course."

Madison rubbed her stomach. "Yum. Now, how is that new grandbaby of yours?"

"The most beautiful baby on God's green earth." Mrs. Mayberry beamed. "Now, shoo. I'm busy." She winked.

Madison touched Ashton's arm. "May I speak with you a moment?"

"Of course. Walk with me to my office."

"It's concerning the keys in the laundry room. Do you have a second one to the studio?"

"Yes. It's there on the holder." She paced toward the keys on the wall mount and fingered through them. "Hmm. That's strange. It's not here."

A chill snaked down Madison's spine. Whoever entered the studio knew to look in the laundry room for the extra one. Perhaps someone who worked at the inn? No way Mrs. Mayberry or Tony would've wanted to come into the little workshop. Who then?

Ashton turned to Madison and gripped her shoulder. "What's going on?"

"Someone broke into the studio." Madison wiped her clammy hand down her jeans.

"Oh, no. Is anything missing?"

"No, but they destroyed my first stained-glass project. I found the suncatcher broken in pieces on the worktable. And what's worse, whoever the person is must still have the key."

"Don't worry. I'll call a locksmith, and then James and I will file the report online."

"I always lock the studio. You were so gracious to allow me to use it … " Tears welled up in her eyes, and she tamped them down.

"The break-in is not your fault. I'm concerned for your safety. And perhaps that of the guests at the inn." Ashton slipped her cell phone out of her pocket. "I'll call a locksmith now. Do you know of anyone who'd want to do this to you?"

Madison started to share her suspicions of both

Victoria and Josh, but she shook her head instead. As Micah had indicated, the evidence was not in, and both deserved the benefit of doubt.

"From now on, I'll keep the extra key in the safe."

Was the break-in a warning meant to scare her? Madison tossed her head. Ha. Took a lot more than that to frighten her. The destruction of her craft only made her more determined to find out who did it.

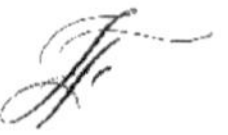

"For all have sinned and fall short of the glory of God, and all are justified freely by his grace through the redemption that came by Christ Jesus." Pastor Ethridge closed his Bible. "My friends, if you haven't availed yourself of Jesus's free gift of salvation, today is your day. Go in peace."

Madison stuck the bulletin in her purse, rose from the pew, and followed Micah into the aisle. The few times she'd attended church, the pastor's words had evoked questions that haunted her. Was she a sinner like the Bible said? Did God's Son really take the death penalty that was due her? Did she need a Savor like the pastor said? She really wasn't that bad of a person.

Micah grasped her hand as they walked out the church sanctuary door.

On the front porch, Pastor Ethridge smiled.

Micah cleared his throat. "We had a setback with the purchase of The Caring Center. The owner took the house off the market."

The pastor frowned. "I'm so sorry. Not a problem, though. I'll call both ministries and ask them to put a hold on the funds. I'm sure you'll find another property." He smiled. "Maybe God has in mind a better deal than the first."

"Yes, perhaps." Micah rested his hand on Madison's waist as they walked to his car.

"I agree with him. Another house will turn up soon," she said.

A bird tweeted in a nearby tree, heralding his joy of another day on earth. Plain as if Ashton stood next to her, Madison remembered her words. *The day will come when you'll have questions about God.*

Micah held the passenger door for her. "Did you talk to Ashton about the key?"

She nodded. "She kept the second key in the laundry room. When we looked, it was gone. Ashton changed the locks and made an online police report. She's as concerned as I am."

Settling in the driver's seat, he glanced over his shoulder to the cooler in the backseat. "How about we go to the city park again to enjoy that lunch?"

"And forget about intruders, and girls with crushes, and men who filed lawsuits, and people with binoculars who keep marked up pictures of you." Madison leaned against the headrest and closed her eyes, glad Micah drove.

"Wow, since you put it that way…" Micah teased.

Madison turned her head to look at him and smiled. "Pastor's message raised a lot of questions in my mind this morning."

Micah's broad, warm hand slid over hers. "Give me a chance to tackle a few."

Of the Christians she knew, she trusted Ashton and Micah to clarify the concerns she had—the doubts that lingered.

Micah parked and grabbed the cooler out of the back. "Let's walk the path farther into the woods. There're some tables closer to the lake."

The sun shining, bees bumbling among flowering plants, the aroma of wildflowers—she couldn't ask for a better day. Last week's worries seemed to be buried in the past.

"How about here?" Micah plopped the cooler on a wooden picnic table next to the shimmering water. A dragonfly explored a patch of water lilies gracing the surface.

"This spot couldn't be more perfect." She retrieved the sandwiches and potato salad, and then two bottles of lemonade and a couple of paper plates.

"Those whole wheat sandwiches with chicken are calling me." He grasped her hand and prayed.

Madison savored her sandwich and gazed beyond the lake to a stand of maples creating flickering shadows on the ground. "Remember the day we talked about how nature reflected the attributes of God?"

"Yeah, about how the skies alone can point to the Creator."

"I do believe there is a God, but how can we get to know Him?"

"Remember when Pastor read that scripture which said we're all sinners?"

"Yes, but I haven't murdered anyone or stolen anything."

He sipped his drink. "Even one microscopic sin can keep us from entering into God's presence."

She grasped her waist. "You mean like telling a little bitty lie, or thinking only one bad thought? That seems rather picky. He must be a demanding God."

Micah nodded. "Yes, because He's perfect. We have to answer for every little wrong thing we do. But the good news is, God's holy Son paid the price for the sins we commit. All we have to do is honestly regret what we did, ask Him to forgive us, and accept His gift of salvation. And then we have free access to the Father."

She crinkled her nose. "That sounds too easy."

"Perhaps you're right, but the Creator makes the rules, not me."

For moments, Madison mulled over her questions. "If He's perfect, then He must know what He's talking about." Yearning prodded and nudged her. She needed a Savior like that. "I want the Father to forgive me."

Micah's eyes glistened. He reached for her hand again. "Would you like me to help you pray?"

Desire for a Savior rolled through her soul like hot lava from a volcano. "More than I can say."

Later in the afternoon, she sat next to Micah on a fallen, cedar log, dangling her toes in the cool water. "I feel at peace, grounded. Is that how it was for you when you first trusted the Lord?" she whispered.

"You're fortunate. For me, those feelings came later on. At first, I wanted to validate the truth by reading more of God's message to people." He dug in his jeans pocket and pulled out a small book. "This is yours. The Holy Bible."

She leaned nearer to kiss his prickly cheek. "Thank you. I've never known anyone like you."

As the sun grew closer to the horizon, he stood. "We'd better start back."

"I wish this day could last forever."

"Me, too." He juggled the cooler as they hiked down

the path.

At the car, Madison breathed deeply and faced the tall, wide-shouldered guy. "I hope there won't be any more disturbing incidents." She gave a sardonic laugh. Who was she kidding?

As she climbed in the car, her phone rang. She checked the screen. Josh.

Not again.

And so soon after the vandalism.

She clicked the red hang-up button.

If Josh had ruined her project, she'd never forgive him.

Then she sat up straight. Hadn't God forgiven her for her sins? Would He require her to forgive Josh?

Chapter Eighteen

Monday afternoon, Madison scrubbed the toilet in room nine, the last of the day's assignments. A smile crept to her lips. Weird because scouring commodes wasn't her favorite pastime. But this day was different.

Before, her existence seemed muddled, as if she couldn't see the road ahead. Now, like a veil had lifted, her life began to make sense. For the first time, she knew who she was and to Whom she belonged.

Madison ambled down the stairs and to Ashton's office. She couldn't wait to tell her friend the news.

At the open door, Ashton waved her in. "I've got the key to your studio. The locksmith showed up soon after I called." She passed her a small envelope in the shape of the key. "James and I made the police report, as well."

"What did they say?"

"They have a record of the incident. They said if there's a next time, call the police immediately and take a picture of the evidence."

"I pray there's no next time." Madison removed the key from the paper and hooked it on her keychain with Be Still and Know engraved on the front.

Ashton leaned nearer and peered into Madison's eyes. "You seem in a good mood today."

Madison slipped into her usual chair next to the desk. "Something happened yesterday."

Ashton smiled and gave her a thumbs up. "Micah finally kissed you."

A belly laugh bubbled up. "Well, almost, but that's another story. No, something very different although it does involve Micah."

Ashton folded her hands, her eyes wide. "He asked you to marry him. I want to see your ring."

"Be quiet a minute, and I'll tell you." Madison grinned at her friend. "Yesterday, Micah and I went to church."

"I saw you."

"Then you heard the message Pastor gave."

Ashton opened her eyes wide. "Yessss."

"Micah and I took a picnic lunch to the park and talked. A lot."

"I'm listening."

"I gave my life to the Lord yesterday. Micah helped me pray."

Ashton jumped up and wrapped her in a bear hug. "I'm so grateful."

"He gave me a little Bible until I can get a larger one." She patted her jeans pocket.

Ashton returned to her chair. "I'm not saying life will be perfect now, but you have Someone who'll see you through." She swiped a tear from her cheek. "God answered a prayer I've asked of Him for a long time."

"I have a lot to learn, though." Madison stood. "Gotta try out my new key to the studio. Making a new design is at the top of my list."

At the studio's door, Madison slipped her key into the shiny, new lock which rotated perfectly to the right. Her equipment, the shelves and tables, all seemed undisturbed. Since she still had plenty of time left in the day, why not start a new project? She'd change the color scheme to golds and browns. She had ample supplies—plastic gloves, brushes, paper for drawing patterns, project boards, glass, and a square ruler.

She sketched a pattern, a butterfly drinking nectar from a clump of small flowers.

The quietness overwhelmed her after a few moments, and Micah's words haunted her. *Sometimes it's the silence that can be most worrying.*

She tiptoed to the window and looked out. No one was outside in the yard. She raked a hand through her hair. She was letting her imagination spook her. Taking a deep breath, she returned to her work. "God, please watch over Micah and me."

She shook her head and picked up her pencil again. One more time, she turned her attention to the window. What was wrong with her?

A tap sounded. Madison crept to the door and inched it open, perspiration forming on her forehead. Victoria stood, her back to her, staring at the deck … or was she purposely turned to keep a weapon hidden from view.

Madison gripped the door to stop her racing heart. "What do you want?" She hated the clipped tone.

The woman swung around. "Madison, is everything okay?" Ashton, a frown on her face, stared at her.

"It's you. I thought you were… " Madison let out a long breath. "I'm sorry. I overreacted. I suppose I'm jumpy this afternoon."

"Sorry I startled you. If you haven't eaten, come to

the dining room tonight. Tony's trying his hand at Mexican food. We're having a fiesta."

Madison clamped her fingers over her heart, trying to still the wild beating. "Th … thanks. I'll be there shortly."

Having dinner at the inn's dining room, surrounded by guests and servers, sounded safe. Her fears had been unfounded, but they'd unsettled her. She couldn't allow alarm to control her just because she and Micah had experienced several different frightening scenarios. She had to get a grip. Returning to the studio to work on her project after dinner would prove she hadn't given in to her nerves.

Madison patted her full stomach. Ashton was right. Tony had prepared a delicious fiesta. In the past, enchiladas *Suizas* and chalupas hadn't played a part in Madison's usual diet, but now she couldn't wait to ask Micah if he liked Mexican food. The aroma of cilantro, tomatoes, and onions followed her as she left the inn's dining room through the door to the deck.

The inn's backyard wasn't well lit, though, at times, James turned on the tiki lights. The moon offered no illumination with the layer of clouds blanketing the sky. Madison lifted her chin and headed down the path toward the studio. She passed the elm tree and Aunt Gina's grave and turned right, off the path, to the workshop.

As a child, Madison was never one to call her mom to investigate the area under the bed for the bogie man.

She had few childhood fears, so why start now? She opened the door with her key and switched on the lights.

The bulb inside the overhead fixture flashed then went dark.

No problem. She clicked on the lamp over the worktable. Plenty of light illuminated part of the studio—enough to continue working on her butterfly project. Next, she pulled out her phone and texted Ashton. James wouldn't mind changing the bulb in the morning.

Madison shuffled through her papers and located the copies she needed. Picking up her scissors, she cut out the shapes and situated them on the glass.

After gluing them down, she positioned her glass cutter.

Thirty minutes later, she glanced toward the window. No terror struck her heart tonight and no phantom peered in. She sighed. Making progress on her project felt good.

A knock sounded on her door. She stood to answer. Surely, Ashton wouldn't have sent James to change the bulbs so late in the evening.

"Coming." Madison opened the door a crack, and then she gripped her hands into tight balls. "What are you doing here?"

Chapter Nineteen

Anger and then fear gripped Madison, and her hands turned to ice. "Josh, you're the last person I ever expected to see tonight."

Her ex-husband, shoulders slumped, held empty hands toward her. "Madison, I need to talk. May I come in?"

No. She didn't trust him, couldn't trust him. Not in the light of everything that had happened. She pushed the door shut and fastened the lock. "We have nothing to talk about," she hollered through the closed door. Let him think that her refusal to see him had to do with anger toward him and not the real reason: complete and utter terror.

She leaned her back against the door, her hands clasped behind her to keep them from shaking. Without another entrance, she'd trapped herself inside. But outside, there was a lot of space for him to harm her without anyone seeing.

"Madison. Please. I only want to talk for a moment. I need to beg your forgiveness. To set things straight." His muffled voice filtered through.

She glanced toward the ceiling as if God would write

an answer there. "You can speak to me through the door."

"Please, Madison. We were husband and wife for a while. If that meant anything at all to you, please give me the opportunity to talk to you."

She'd heard this tone a couple of times during their short marriage. When he drank, he became violent. In his sobriety, the guilt ate at him, and he always sought redemption from her. "Have you been drinking?"

"No. I promise. I haven't had a drop in weeks. Are you afraid of me? I know I was rotten to you, and more so, when I drank, and I'm sorry. Those days are over. I will never …"

Madison closed her eyes and lifted a prayer to God for her safety. She unlocked the door and opened the protective barrier a crack.

Instead of pushing through as she feared, Josh gazed at her with a pained expression. "I promise I'm not here for any other reason than to say I'm sorry. I would never lay a hand on you now."

Like he did once when he shoved her in a drunken rage. She nodded, opened the door wider, and took two steps backward.

Josh stepped into the studio. He moved around as if he'd never seen the place—not that he should have unless he'd been the one to steal the key. He paused by her table and fingered the paper and materials without moving them. "Stained-glass?" he asked.

Madison nodded.

"When we were together, you mentioned you wanted to take up the hobby. I'm glad you have."

Madison frowned at him. "How did you know I was here in this building?"

"I was in the inn, and I asked a woman ..."

"Ashton?"

"No. No. I've never seen her before. I thought she was a new employee, but you know, she could have been a guest. She knew who you were and told me I could probably find you out here."

"So, this is the absolute first time you've set foot in here?"

He blinked as if trying to decode her words. "I've never been in here before. What's this about?" He moved toward her, reaching for her.

Madison stepped backward, holding her hands outward to brace against his advances, whatever they might be. "You said that you were here to tell me you're sorry. This isn't a kiss and make up moment, Josh. This is a moment where we decide that our past is best left there, and we should go our separate ways once and for all."

Josh still advanced toward her.

Madison stepped back, bumping into her stool and knocking the seat over. "Stay away from me."

Josh blew out a puff of air and dropped his arms. "Look, Madison. I'm only here for one reason. To say how much I regret the way we parted. I wanted to give you a hug for old time's sake."

"You walked away from me."

"I know that. And I'm so sorry. I should never have handled things that way. Our marriage was dying. Both of us knew our vows had been a mistake. I should've faced you—let you know how I was feelings so that we could part friends. I was immature and thoughtless. That's why I'm here: to rectify the mistakes I made in ending our relationship." He scrubbed his hand over his mouth. "Can we be friends and leave it like that?"

Should she believe him? Everyone deserved a second chance? God had given her one, hadn't He? "I forgive you and want to believe you." She walked to the door and opened it. "Something inside tells me not to trust you. I want to believe it's only because of our past experience. I'll have to see. Maybe … someday."

Josh walked through the door. "I can accept that for now."

Madison locked the door against the black night and leaned against the hard surface. Accepting his apology would heal part of the enmity which had dug into her heart, chipping away her peace. But did she really believe he'd spoken sincerely?

She had no idea who she could trust short of Ashton and Micah.

She had some potent bear spray she'd put away. The time had come to pull it out and keep it on her at all times. Why not? Micah seemed to always carry his gun.

Micah munched the hotdog, savoring the mustard and sauerkraut he'd piled on. The new food stand near the pier got his approval. After the last bite, he tossed the paper wrapper in the receptacle. Getting away from the store during lunch invigorated him.

The seagulls' calls and the warm, salty air reminded him of Who created this day and Who had a purpose for him. Micah whispered his prayer into the wind. "Lord, guide my steps as I walk into the future." Whatever lay ahead, God was in charge.

Since Karina would need a break, Micah walked the fifty yards to the store and climbed the stairs. Before reaching the store, he pulled out his phone and dialed Madison.

He was getting used to seeing her daily, and he didn't want to lose the opportunity to do so later.

When she answered, the sound of his name on her lips enticing him, he asked one question. "Dinner?"

"Dinner." She answered back.

"At my place?" he continued.

"At your place?" Her question mirrored his. "We have two problems there. You can't cook, and your kitchen is too small."

He laughed. "Did I mention I'd swing by the new pizza place downtown and get takeout on my way home from work?"

"Micah Collins. That's an offer I can't turn down."

"See you later." He hung up and entered the store.

He could get use to conversations like that with her every day of the week.

The aroma of fresh pizza filled the air in Micah's apartment. He opened the door at the knock.

Madison's hair, shoulder length, touchable, and lush, and her luminous blue eyes elevated his pulse, no matter how hard he tried to stay calm. Her turquoise blouse and perfectly-fitting skinny jeans sent a message to his heart. He blinked. He'd allowed Madison to stand on his doorstep while he gawked at her. "Come in."

She laughed. "I wondered if you were going to invite

me in."

"Sorry. I suppose I was staring. You look amazing."

She grinned. "You look—well, very handsome."

Micah fought the desire to wrap his arms around her, draw her close, and discover the feel of her soft, pink lips. *Get ahold of yourself, man.* Madison hadn't come to his apartment so they could make out.

He shook off his musings and pointed to his couch.

Within thirty minutes, most of the pizza had disappeared, and Madison had shared with him her encounter with her ex-husband. He wasn't exactly pleased that the man had shown up in the dead of night to knock on Madison's studio door, but according to her, he'd left without incident after saying what he'd come to say.

Madison gathered the plates and placed them in his miniature kitchen sink.

Micah stacked their glasses on the counter. Eating a meal, clearing dishes with her, felt natural, right. "You're okay about your ex-husband? Do you think he wants to get back together?"

Madison firmed her lips. "If he does, he's sadly mistaken. I'm glad we no longer have unfinished business between us, but I would never want to go back to him."

"Would you think me presumptuous for saying I'm glad you don't?"

"No. I'm happy your feel that way. But I'm weary of being frightened, worried about what will come next."

He smiled. "Only this morning, I read a scripture about fear. I'll admit that it seemed fit for me because I had an incident with Bates. He signed up for fishing lessons after buying a new rod and reel. He made no bones about doing it so I could go fishing with him, and he invited us both to the lesson."

"I won't let you go out there alone, Micah."

He touched a tendril of her hair and held it in his fingers before releasing it. "Thank you for that. The Bible says God doesn't make us afraid, but gives us power, love, and a sound mind. Truth you can believe."

"That is very comforting."

"And it spoke toward something else that I've been afraid to do. I want to share with you something that's percolated in the back of my mind." He grasped her hands. "I'm thinking the time has come to reestablish my practice." Yet now, he hoped Madison would be at his side.

Madison's eyes lit with encouragement. "I love the idea."

Chapter Twenty

Madison smothered a yawn as she unlocked the studio. After staying up half the night reading her Bible, she hadn't slept much. Like perusing a fascinating novel, she couldn't put the book down. The stories of King David, Samson, and Moses had fascinated her. Two cups of coffee this morning hadn't been enough.

She flipped the switch, and the bulb bathed the area in light. "Thank you, James," she mumbled. A quick look around the studio to make sure no intruders had showed up in the night and she'd return to her duties cleaning the guest rooms.

The studio looked the same as when she'd left yesterday. Why was she concerned someone had broken in? She ran her finger over the new lock the locksmith had changed a couple of days ago. Secure. Nothing to worry about. She could begin her day's work without concern.

Madison secured the studio door and headed for the kitchen entrance to the inn.

Mrs. Mayberry lugged a large plastic garbage bag out the exit.

Madison picked up her pace. "Let me take it to the

dumpster for you."

Mrs. Mayberry's smile said how grateful she felt. "That would be wonderful, Madison. I need to attend to some cinnamon buns in the oven."

The dumpster sat near a clump of trees next to a dirt road where the city emptied the container every other week.

Madison hauled the heavy bag within a few feet of the large garbage bin. She hoisted up the awkward sack, ready to toss the bundle inside.

"Can I help?"

Madison yelped and dropped the bag to the ground.

Mr. Ford stood on the other side of the container closer to the trees and stepped toward the dumpster. He wore a fishing hat that dropped over his brow. Sunglasses covered his eyes, and the pockets on the fishing vest were filled with tackle. He carried a fly rod.

Madison took a step back. What did he want? She held her breath.

"The bag is almost as big as you are." He inched closer.

She held her hand up in a stop position. "Stay away. You'll get an eye full of something worse than pepper spray."

"Whoa. Wait, little lady. I don't mean any harm. I thought we were friends."

"Yeah, sure." She gulped and stared at the guy only eight feet away on the other side of the dumpster. "What do you want, Mr. Ford?"

"Isn't it obvious? I saw you with the bag, and I wanted to help."

Madison slipped her finger in her pocket and fingered the can of spray. "I'm fine. Thank you."

"Then I'll be on my way. Lots of fish out there waiting for me, you know."

"So which is it, Mr. Ford? Are you a detective or a fisherman?"

"Can't I be both?" He smiled an almost fatherly smile. "I don't work around the clock."

"But can't *she* get into trouble while you're fishing?"

"She?" He raised his brows.

Madison looked behind her. "Yes, *she.* You know," she lowered her voice, "Victoria."

Light dawned in his eyes. "Yes. Yes." He shook his head. "Of course, she can, but she's a big girl. I can't stop her from doing anything, but I can report on it when I learn what she's done."

Madison straightened. "Her parents are paying you simply to report on her behavior? Wouldn't they want you to intervene if she's done something criminal."

He titled his head. "Has she done something I should know about?"

"Mr. Ford, why did you have a picture of Micah Collins on your desk?" She tightened her grip on the spray, readying to bring it forth.

"So you saw that, did you?" He laughed. Before she could move her hand, he was near her. "Let's just say that the picture is what brought me to Cranberry Cove."

Madison trembled.

Ford leaned away from her. "You're in no danger from me, but Micah … That man's got trouble on his back, and he doesn't even know it. Now, if you'll excuse me, I've got a fish to catch." He tipped the brim of his hat with his hand and hurried away.

Madison swiped a stringy strand of hair from her eyes and unlocked the studio door. She was a mess after cleaning not only the rooms but the refrigerator and freezer. Calling Micah and reporting her conversation with Ford had been on her must-do list all day, but Mrs. Mayberry had it in mind that she needed to update the menus. How could she have said no to her? When Mrs. Mayberry admitted her computer skills were lacking, creating an entire month's menu became even more taxing. Trying to get her own work completed to find time to call Micah had been near impossible with Mrs. Mayberry seeking her out to ask questions about the computer.

Madison brushed the bits of goo from leftovers in the fridge off her jeans. She couldn't wait to get home and take a shower.

And to call Micah.

She shook her head. Every time something happened, she called him or ran to tell him. Nothing had occurred so far. Why worry him needlessly? Instead, she'd wait until she saw him to share Mr. Ford's warning.

A soft rap on the door sounded like Ashton's knock, but why didn't she walk in afterward like her boss usually did?

She peeked out the door.

Victoria stood outside. "May I come in? I'd like to chat for a moment."

Madison stepped back and opened the door wider. "Yes, of course. Please come in."

The woman stuck out her hand. "I'm not sure if you

would remember me. I'm Victoria."

Madison pointed to a stool. "Yes, I remember. Please take a seat if you'd like."

Victoria sat and seemed to be scrutinizing Madison.

"How are you enjoying your vacation? Cranberry Cove is one of our best kept secrets in Washington state." Madison slipped onto a stool adjacent to Victoria.

"I love it here." She flipped a long strand of hair off her shoulders making Madison more aware of her own messy appearance.

"Wonderful. Have you visited the lighthouse or shopped any of the boutiques downtown? I love to travel up the coast a way and have lunch at some of the quaint, seaside restaurants. Best clam chowder you'll get anywhere."

Victoria's gaze never left Madison. The woman seemed to be searching for something. She, no doubt, had questions about Micah's relationship with Madison. "I've toured the lighthouse, and I'll take your other suggestions. I suppose a date takes you there once in a while."

"My friend Micah Collins and I dine at the wharf on occasion and visit the lighthouse. I understand you know him."

"Who told you that?" Victoria lifted up from the stool and paced. "Was it Bates?" She narrowed her eyes. "Or was it your friend Micah?" She placed her hands on her hips. "I suppose that he told you all about me. I lost my breasts and my self-confidence. I cried on his shoulder. He took care of me." She straightened. "He took very good care of me."

Madison stood and placed a hand on Victoria's shoulders. The woman trembled. "Micah told me only that you were an ex-patient of his, nothing more. Do you think Micah would violate his ethics?"

Victoria seemed to hesitate but then she shook her head. "Did he tell you how close we were? How he helped me through a difficult time?" The woman's eyes darkened. "How I wouldn't have made it without him?"

"No, Victoria. Micah wouldn't share your confidences with me. I'm so sorry that you've had to endure what you've gone through. Micah and I are working to open a center that might be helpful to you, where you can come and share your journey and learn from others who have gone through the same thing."

A storm brewed in Victoria's eyes. She slapped Madison's hand away from her. "All I need to know is that Micah loves me."

Madison remained silent, unwilling and unable to share with Victoria what the woman desired to know.

The storm seemed to lift and move away. She went to the door and opened it. "Nice to chat with you, Morgan."

"It's Madison."

"Oh, yes. Madison. I apologize." She smiled. "You need to take care." She closed the door with a soft click.

A chill worked its way up Madison's spine and onto her neck. Had Victoria just threatened her?

Chapter Twenty-One

The next day, Madison helped Mrs. Mayberry set out the fruit tray and scones. When Tony asked her to take breakfast orders, she couldn't say no. The coffeepots in the thermal carafe waited on the side table along with cream and sugar.

Guests began streaming in, possibly summoned by the delicious aroma of bacon, smoked sausage, and ham filling the dining room.

Pad and pencil in hand, Madison went to the table nearest the window and took their egg and meat order. After turning in the guests' breakfast request, she headed to the table closest to the kitchen.

"Can a man get a cup of coffee around here?"

She turned to the person whose voice she knew well. "Good morning, Micah. You came to the right place."

"I had to make a visit to Blake's second store about a mile from the inn and thought I'd drop in." He glanced around the room.

"Sit at one of the cleared tables. Would you like some breakfast?"

He lifted his hand. "Just coffee is fine."

Madison set a cup of steaming coffee in front of him

along with cream and sugar. "I'll sit down with you as soon as I can."

Twenty minutes later and the dining room empty, she slipped down in the chair opposite Micah.

"I don't mean to keep you from your duties."

"No problem. I'm glad you came in. I'd like to talk to you about Mr. Ford."

Micah groaned. "Is he still around?" He sipped his coffee.

"Yes. He approached me by the dumpsters. He seemed friendly enough, but when I asked him why, if he was here for Victoria, did he have that picture of you, he said the picture is what brought him here, and he indicated that you might be in trouble."

Micah scratched his head. "Did he say what kind of trouble?"

She shook her head. "Honestly, now, I'm wondering if he thinks you've done something to Victoria. In fact, she came to me yesterday."

Micah sat up. "Just saying hello, I hope."

Madison sighed. "I'm afraid she was staking out her territory, though she seems unsure about where you stand. She's clearly infatuated with you in an abnormal sort of way." She scooted closer to Micah and lowered her voice. "Do you think that Victoria is delusional?"

Micah started out the window before looking Madison in the eyes. "No. I don't believe she is. High strung, prone to flights of fancy, demanding, temperamental, yes. Delusional, no. Did she appear that way to you?"

Madison thought on the question for a moment. No, but something had been driving the woman, something beyond her own desires. "I wondered for a moment if she had indicated a relationship with you during the treatment. That would explain Mr. Ford's possession of your picture. Ford might be following you to determine if you and Victoria are continuing to see each other."

"Madison." Micah breathed out her name. "I have never seen that woman for anything but her medical treatment." Hurt settled over his features. "My wife was alive through the course of that treatment. Do you think I would have cheated on her? I was trying my best to encourage Ellen and keep her alive while treating patients who might be at death's door themselves. That's why I came here, to get away from the reminders. Victoria was a reminder."

Madison placed her hand on top of his. "I believe you, but temperamental women sometimes blur the edges of honesty to get what they want."

Micah nodded. "Point taken."

"And the lawsuit was the only trouble you had, right? After it settled, there was nothing else?"

"Nothing," he assured.

Micah crossed his arms over his chest. "I want you to be careful around Victoria. She lashes out in anger at times. She'll settle down soon enough, but it's part of that spoiled-child syndrome. I once told her when she attacked her mother in my office that one day, her blind fury was going to cause her to do something she'd regret."

Madison sat back in her chair. "She attacked her mother?"

"Flew at her in a rage when her mother sided with me on a course of treatment. I can't go into it here, just to say that Victoria didn't see eye to eye with me or her mother. I stepped in or her mother might have fallen. Victoria got her way because her father gives her everything."

Madison tapped her fingers on the table. "And maybe Mr. Ford is here because her father intends on giving you to her as well."

Micah stretched his tired shoulders and locked the front door to the store. Working late on inventory wore him out, but he had to perform the task while the store was empty of customers.

Frustration and anger bugged him every time he thought of Ford. What was the man after? Why didn't he just come out and ask for it? If he could only get his hands on the guy for worrying Madison…

He took the stairs down to the wharf parking lot.

A fog rolled off of the waters as the temperature had dropped, clashing with the waters earlier warmed by the sunlight.

In the midst, he thought he saw movement. As if he hadn't spied anything, Micah continued on. He let a whistled tune split his lips as he dug into his pocket for his car keys and approached his car.

He pushed the button to unlock his vehicle, and as he went to sit inside, he looked in the direction of the movement.

Ford leaned against the wall near the stairs, his intent gaze on Micah.

Micah looked away as if not seeing him, but he was tired of this *I Spy* game. He raised up, purposefully snapped his fingers, and reversed course up the stairs again. He'd warn the guy to leave him and Madison alone.

Ford remained in his position, obviously unaware that Micah had seen him.

Micah reached the store's door, fumbled with his keys to complete the ruse, and then turned. "Mr. Ford?" He made his way toward the detective.

As if he'd not heard Micah, the man turned and walked through the corridor between a souvenir shop and the military museum.

"Mr. Ford." Micah gained on him.

The man turned a corner and disappeared into the dark night.

Micah continued on, finding himself in complete darkness at the backside of the wharf. Had Ford led him here on purpose because there were no cameras, no lights to shine upon his misdeeds.

Ford turned. "Dr. Collins, to what do I owe the pleasure?"

Micah caught up with him. "I'm tired of your meddling. Tell me the reason you're here."

The guy raised two hands in front of his chest. "Have I done anything to harm you in any way?"

Micah growled and ignored the stalling tactic. "What do you want with me?"

Ford inched away from the confrontation. "Look, I can't say anything right now."

Micah shook his head and scowled. "Approach Madison Mitchell one more time, and we'll finish this conversation. And what did you mean by telling her that I have trouble?"

Ford's shoulders relaxed. "All I can say to you is that not all is as it seems. You're in danger, Dr. Collins. Your trust in certain people could get you killed."

Chapter Twenty-Two

The next day, Micah lowered into his swivel chair and switched his calendar to the first day of July. He'd had a sleepless night rethinking his confrontation with Ford.

An advertisement sitting on the edge of his desk featured one of his favorites—fresh caught salmon—at The Wharf. He'd ask Madison to dinner soon.

The phone rang, and Micah picked it up on the second ring.

"This is Janette from Town and Country Realty. Can you and your ministry partner meet with me this afternoon at my office so I can take you to look at a property in downtown Cranberry Cove? I believe it's exactly what you're looking for."

Micah pumped his fist in a victory cheer. "You bet. That's wonderful. Thanks."

She gave him the address and hung up.

Five seconds later, Micah dialed Madison, his heart tapping a fast beat. "Are you ready for some good news for once?"

"For sure. What ya got?" She laughed.

"Meet Janette and me at two this afternoon at her

office. She has a location for us to look at."

"I'll be there."

He pictured her wide grin and glistening eyes. "Looks like the center is on the way to opening its doors."

Micah held the door for Janette and Madison as they walked out of the downtown building onto the sidewalk.

Janette motioned toward the old, but well-preserved edifice set between the dry cleaners and the drug store. "The location has its advantages because the building is situated in the center of Cranberry Cove. Of course, it's a storefront instead of a house."

Micah glanced toward Madison to see her reaction. Did she like the idea of opening The Caring Center in a seventy-five-year-old building as much as he?

Madison paused on the sidewalk and stared at the property. "If Cranberry Cove was a large city like Tacoma or Seattle, I don't believe this would work—especially with parking or a possible long drive from home. But in our town, we have little traffic. I certainly think it's feasible."

"And the asking price is considerably less than the last house we considered," Micah said.

Janette locked the front door with her master key. "The commercial space is smaller than the house, but you don't have the acreage or the upkeep on the acreage as well. Also, the upkeep and cleaning here would be less for you. And you don't have to seek a change in zoning from residential to commercial for the property. That's a huge savings."

Micah nodded. "You're right. Here we have a bathroom in the back, a small area we can use for individual counseling, and a larger room for group sessions. I think it's perfect."

"Don't forget the little kitchen with the fridge, sink, and space for a microwave." Madison clasped her hands under her chin. "I think we've found our home for The Caring Center."

Janette glanced at the spec sheet on her clipboard. "You won't need quite as large of an escrow to contract on this property as the last."

Micah lifted his gaze upward. "We'll be paying cash, so I'd like to make an offer below list price."

"Cash does talk in this market, Micah. They might make a counter offer or stand firm, but there's no harm in trying," Janette advised.

"We'll leave that in the Lord's hands."

Janette gathered her papers into her briefcase. "What are we waiting for? Let's go to the office and make an offer."

Outside the realty office, Madison pressed her hand to her chest, fingers splayed. "Congratulations, Micah. You did it. The Caring Center will be open soon."

"You deserve half the credit." He kissed her hand. "After I call Pastor Ethridge, let's go celebrate. You got any ideas."

"Mount Williams, about twenty miles northwest of here, has one of the most gorgeous views of the bay. We can take snacks and drinks and drive most of the way. Then there's a short hike to the lookout point."

"I like the idea." Micah opened the door to his car, and she stepped in.

Forty-five minutes later and the call to Pastor Ethridge done, Madison rolled down the window and allowed the cool breeze to flow through her hair as they traveled up in elevation. "I can't imagine a more serene view." High above the coast, layers and layers of evergreen trees graced the downward slope.

They pulled off on a side road at the sign with *scenic view—three miles*, drove up the road to the parking lot, and got out.

Micah leaned against the metal railing bordering the downward slope. "The view of the water and a mountain range beyond steals my breath."

Something else stole Madison's breath. Merely looking at the good-looking man with wide, masculine shoulders increased her pulse.

He leaned nearer, only inches from her. "Do I have permission … " he whispered.

"Um, hum." Madison lifted her face and slipped her arms around Micah. What more could she ask for?

He placed his lips on hers, causing Madison to forget that anything or anyone existed besides the two of them. Then an uncomfortable notion struck, and she moved away. "Are you ready, Micah? Ready for this? I mean, what about Ellen?"

Micah rubbed his forehead. "Ellen is enjoying eternity. There's nothing I can do to change the loss of my wife. She would want me to find someone else." He bent to kiss her nose. "I loved her dearly, but I need to move on." He held out his left ring finger. "For a long while after her death, I wore my wedding ring. A few months before I met you, I'd taken the band off. For me, the act symbolized the end of my marriage."

"I understand." Madison stood on tiptoes and slipped her arms around him again. "I'm grateful you want to move in my direction." She lifted her lips to kiss his, this time with no interruptions.

Micah tightened his arms around her waist, his lips moving more passionately on hers. Then he stepped back and raked his hand through his hair. "I need to back off. I don't want to get too … er … enthusiastic about kissing you. I might find myself in trouble."

She ran her hand down his cheek and laughed. "I've adopted new standards I never had before—thanks to you."

"I think when the Lord comes into a person's life, that person is changed by the Holy Spirit."

"I've got a lot to learn," Madison said.

"You will. Give it time."

Madison gazed at the view once more. "Have you decided when you're going into medicine again."

"Soon." Micah scrubbed a hand over his mouth and gazed toward the ocean. "I've considered opening an office in Cranberry Cove instead of Sacramento."

Micah settling in Cranberry Cove? Her stomach fluttered like a boat's sails flapping in the breeze. "Would you specialize in oncology again?"

He shook his head. "Since I don't have access to a hospital in Cranberry Cove, I thought about internal medicine."

"Is it feasible to switch your focus to something different from what you did before?"

"Yes, I trained as an internal medicine doctor before

I specialized in women's health." He grinned. "Of course, I'll need to visit with Janette again. What do you think?"

"I love the idea." Madison took a few steps toward the fence, gazing at the view of the bay hundreds of feet below. Micah solidifying his plans, her life more grounded than ever before. Life had begun to fall into place. Now, if only Victoria and Mr. Ford would return home.

Chapter Twenty-Three

The next Monday, Madison stood next to the curb and looked up to the new sign *The Caring Center* across the top of the building. She and Micah had arrived together, but she'd lingered outside to take it all in.

Micah's work on setting up the legalities with the non-profit after he visualized his dream and put it in motion had allowed them to move quickly. Also, Janette had worked a deal with the current owners of the storefront. With full cash deposited in the realtor's escrow and awaiting inspection and The Caring Centers signing off on all contingency matters covered in the contract, they would pay rent for the two weeks' pending the close on the sale.

She smiled as she glanced at the door leading inside. Micah had suggested they paint the panels forest green, the symbol for hope and new beginnings.

She lingered a moment, peeking through the glass windows. Already, she loved watching the morning sunshine flood the front room.

Blake Sloan and Ashton's husband, James, pushed a donated couch into place at one end of the space. Micah and Pastor Ethridge set up folding chairs nearby. In a prominent spot, Mrs. Ethridge hung a picture of Jesus carrying a lamb on His shoulders.

Madison couldn't help humming a tune she'd heard at church.

On the other side of the window, Ashton tapped on the glass and beckoned for Madison to come inside.

She entered and laid a hand over her heart. "I can't believe the day is almost here. The Caring Center will be in business in another two weeks. We couldn't have done all the work without your help."

Micah joined her. "We still need to devise a schedule, recruit a few more volunteers, and advertise the facility locally and in the general area. Pastor Ethridge did a great job of designing the program. His input and knowledge of small groups and individual counseling has proved invaluable. The individual's seeking help here will benefit from his volunteer counseling as well as the other pastors from the area who donated their time." Micah nodded toward the pastor.

Madison smiled. "I'm looking forward to our prayer session at the church tomorrow afternoon after Sunday service."

"I'll be there." Ashton glanced at her watch. "Guess I getter go. Mom Atwood has kept my toddler almost all day."

Micah turned to the others. "I hope the rest of you can stay for pizza. It's the least we can do to thank you."

Two hours later and every piece of four pizzas devoured, Madison waved as the last volunteers left. She gave Micah a high-five. "You deserve a big thank you. The Caring Center wouldn't be possible if it wasn't for your initiative."

"And your help." He nuzzled her cheek.

"You're sweet, Micah Collins, and I intend to do whatever else is necessary to get this place going."

Micah snapped the front door lock, and they headed to his vehicle. At his car in the lot behind the store, he grasped her hands. "I pray we won't hear any more from Ford. And Victoria for that matter."

"Hopefully not. And now, all you need to do is find another property for your medical office."

"I have a feeling Janette will do her magic again."

"She will." Madison grinned. "Guess I better get back to the inn. I need to finish up a few things, and then I have my art class tonight."

Micah drove down Main and turned on the road toward the inn. "I suppose I'll have to wait one whole day until I see you again."

"Good afternoon, Janette." Micah gripped the phone harder. "You found us the perfect spot for the center, but now I've got another real estate need."

"I'm at your service." Janette's cheery voice sent optimism to his heart. "How can I help?"

"I'm looking for a location to accommodate a medical practice. Anywhere in the Cranberry Cove area. I'll explain more when I see you." He took in a cleansing breath. Time for him to share his former life with the people he knew. And give his boss at least a month's notice before he left.

After hanging up, he rose from his office desk and stretched. The Caring Center was almost ready to go, his plans for a medical practice were taking shape, and a beautiful woman had stepped into his life.

A vision of Madison danced in his mind. Her light brown hair, sparkling blue eyes, and small waist and shapely hips—he shook his head. He needed to check on Karina at the front register. About time for her to get off work.

Since the day she'd lost consciousness at the store, Karina had proved to have a strong tolerance toward her chemotherapy. Next time he saw Blake, he'd recommend she receive a raise for her willingness to work long hours without slacking off.

A customer at the register paid and walked out of the store.

"Time for you to go home and take it easy." Micah wiggled his fingers to shoo her away.

Karina's smile widened. "Won't argue with that. See you tomorrow, Micah."

When the next customer approached the register, wading boots in hand, Micah took his credit card and bagged the purchase.

With no more customers in the store, Micah surveyed the display tables and shelves. The t-shirts exhibited by size in little cubby holes on the vertical shelf were messed up, some hanging halfway out. He trekked over to the shelf to straightened them.

Since they were all in disarray, he pulled the entire stack out to refold them. He fumbled with the first t-shirt which came out looking like a jumble of wrinkles. Karina usually did this job. Maybe he should've waited until tomorrow. Face it. He wasn't good at folding stuff.

Trying again, he flipped one sleeve then the other and then the bottom and tucked the first shirt into the small area.

"Here, let me do that."

Micah startled at the nearness of the person to him. The door had not opened.

Had Victoria been inside the store this entire time?

"Silly, didn't your mother teach you how to do this when you were a kid?" She made short work of the task and replaced the shirt on the shelf.

Micah doubted her wealthy mother had taught her either, but he wouldn't make that comment. "Were you in the store?" he asked.

"Yes, looking at your selection ofbathing suits. You have quite a selection." She handed him a t-shirt and touched his arm. "I'm thinking of doing some paddleboarding as well."

Micah almost laughed, but he stayed his humor. "Put your toe in the water first."

She studied him. "Would you like to join me?"

Micah pretended to straighten another shelf, placing space between them. "Did you find a bathing suit you liked. I can ring it up. Will you need a paddleboard, too?" He forced a smile. "I could use the sale. We also have wet suits if you didn't bring one of those. You know, to protect you from the frigid water."

"I would buy a paddleboard from you, but how will I get it home on the plane." Obviously, she missed or ignored his attempt at humor. "I suppose I could have it shipped, but then I'd have two at home." Victoria didn't really see the absurdity in her milling over the choices.

"I wasn't serious." Micah needed to stop this trainwreck.

"Oh," Victoria slipped her arm in his. "Let me show you the bathing suits. You can pick out your favorite for me."

This was getting a little too creepy for his liking. "No, I can't." He unlinked his arm. "If you were really looking to purchase one, the choice should be yours. Unless you're looking for anything else, I'll meet you at the cash register."

She wrapped her arms around her waist and twisted from side to side. Maybe she thought she was being seductive in her short skirt and her shirt with the low V-neck. The pout ruined the effect. "Why are you playing so hard to get?"

Her words went to the depth of him, shaking him. "Victoria…"

She saddled up closer to him. "I know you think about me. I've been told you just needed time after everything that happened in Sacramento."

He hurried down the aisle to stand behind the cash register. "Someone has been telling you lies. You have to know that my only interest in you was as a patient. Your well-being was important to me for that reason only. I wanted to help get you through everything, but there was no further interest on my part."

She stood stock-still for a long moment, and then as if possessed by a demon she reached out to the cabinet of sunglasses encased behind a locked glass. With a piercing scream, she shoved it.

Micah held his breath as the heavy cabinet teetered backward, seemed to hang only by its bottom, to fall forward again, the sunglasses coming off their displays and falling to the bottom of the cabinet. Victoria was fortunate the cabinets glass had not shattered.

Victoria stood in front of it, as if not realizing what she'd done. Then she turned to look at him. "This is not over!" she shrieked. "Not by a longshot. Someone is going to pay for this!" She ran out of the store, slamming the door with a furious shove.

Micah breathed out the air he'd been holding in his lungs and slumped forward. That was the Victoria he'd known during her treatment.

Before he could go around to check the contents in the case, the front door jingled.

Micah headed around the register.

"Good afternoon, Micah."

He skidded to a stop. What were the odds? "Mr. Bates, back for another piece of fishing equipment?"

"No." He smiled a wide grin. "I'm enjoying the rod I purchased last time. In fact, I came to set a time for that lesson." He hitched his thumb toward the door. "Was that Victoria I saw leaving just now. She seemed upset. You didn't break her heart again, did you?"

Micah opened the case housing the sunglasses and began to put the eye wear back on display, checking for breaks or scratches on the lenses. If he found any, he'd be sure to send a bill to Victoria's father. Then Bates's words hit him along with his jovial attitude.

Micah finished his task in short order, closed, and locked the cabinet, and turned to Bates. "You wouldn't happen to know who told your wife's friend that I might be interested in her, would you?"

Bates didn't blink. "You're not? Mary always said she thought the two of you were in love and dancing around the doctor-patient thing. I know the poor gal was devastated when you left town."

"So, you did put her up to coming in here and ..."

"Now, you wait just a minute. I mentioned, probably with a little lapse in judgment, that I thought you might have been waiting for enough time to pass. I did suggest that her being in your vicinity might rekindle anything you might have lost for her while you were gone, but I did not tell her how to act toward you." Bates crossed his arms.

Micah's ire deflated along with his shoulders. "All right. I do owe you an apology. Is there anything else I can help you with?"

"Apology accepted, and I'm not sure how long I'm going to stay, but I would like to take that lesson from you to see if you can teach an old dog some newfangled tricks." Bates smiled and rubbed his nose.

Micah opened up his schedule. "I have something that I'm working on, and I have obligations toward it. When did you expect to leave?"

Bates rubbed his chin now. "The day after I get the lesson. I'm semi-retired. My son, Liam, is running the business. So, whenever you can work me in would be great."

Micah shared a date with him and penciled it in. "You might be interested to learn that the project I'm work on is a center for cancer patients and their families, for those who have lost loved ones to cancer as well. I hope that you'll stay around until after the opening."

Bates rubbed his right eye hard. "Sure. Sure." He cleared his throat. "Remember, bring your friend along. We'll have a great afternoon."

Micah nodded. "Until then, enjoy the fishing."

Chapter Twenty-Four

Micah was pleasantly surprised when Blake came into his store a couple of days later. He motioned for his boss to take a seat. "I have a few things to discuss with you."

Blake sank into the chair and hiked one ankle over his knee. "I apologize for not stopping by lately, but you run this store as well as I could. I appreciate you."

"No problem. You've got a daughter to occupy your time. How's Gracie and your little girl?"

Blake beamed as he pulled out his phone and showed Micah a picture of a newborn wrapped in a pink blanket. "Gracie's fine. God blessed us with a healthy, happy baby. We're still learning how to manage a newborn, but we're both excited to be parents."

"I'm happy for you two." Micah fiddled with a pencil on his desk. From what he knew of Blake, he'd make a great father.

"So, what did you want to discuss? Is Karina working out okay?"

"Yes, she's one of the reasons I wanted to talk to you. But there's another matter first." Micah sat forward in his chair. "I need to give you a month's notice. I'm taking another job in Cranberry Cove."

Blake frowned as he stared at Micah. "Is it anything to do with the store? I'll be happy to make changes to improve your situation if there's a problem."

"No." Micah smiled. "My leaving has nothing to do with the job or the store or Karina. I've enjoyed my work here, but I need to return to my former profession."

"I'm listening." Blake uncrossed his legs and sat straight.

"When I first applied for the job, I listed my last employment as Sacramento General Hospital. I didn't explain what position I had, and you didn't ask. I appreciated that." Micah grinned. "The truth is …" Would Blake believe him when he explained about his former situation? "The truth is … I'm a gynecological oncologist. I worked for a number of years treating women who suffered with cancer."

Blake's mouth dropped open. "What? You're kidding. Then why did you come to Cranberry Cove and work as a manager in a sporting goods store?"

"Long story." Micah explained about Ellen and the lawsuits and needing a break from treating patients. "I'd like to change my practice to internal medicine here in Cranberry Cove. I hope a month will be enough time to find a replacement for my job and to make sure I've met all state requirements to practice here."

"I'm sorry about your wife." Blake stared at his empty hands for a moment and then glanced up. "But I'm grateful you're not leaving us. Cranberry Cove needs another good doctor."

"There's something else. Karina. She's been diagnosed with breast cancer. She's suffering from the treatments, but she needs to keep her job. She's proven to be a loyal employee, working even when she's under the weather, and I'd like to recommend a raise in pay and that I train her to take my position."

Blake rubbed his chin. "I didn't know about her health. I'll be happy to work with her on hours and time off. Based on your advice, a raise will also be coming her way. If you recommend her, she'd be perfect to take your place." He paused, his gaze fixed on Micah as if seeing him for the first time. "To think, a medical doctor, someone far out of his field, has worked for me for the last couple of years."

"A well needed time to regroup—take a breath—for which I thank you. The opportunity has been a lifesaver."

Blake stood and shook Micah's hand. "I'm honored you choose to work for me. You've taken a lot of stress off my plate in the time you've been here, and I appreciate it."

After Blake left, Micah sank into his chair and propped his elbows on the desk. Memories of the first time he established his practice in Sacramento after graduation rolled in like the tide on the Pacific. Funding had presented his first obstacle. Then he'd had to select an office and publicize his new practice. Establishing a list of his patients had come next. All had taken time and persistence. Would he experience the same in Cranberry Cove? Would the town's citizens accept him as a reputable doctor?

Later that afternoon, Micah snapped a photo of the second building and shook hands with Janette. "I can see value in both properties you showed me today."

"Luck was on your side, Dr. Collins. Each location has recently appeared on the market."

Not luck, but the goodness of the Lord.

"The older, single-family house on Maple is perfect. Well maintained and the price is right." She glanced toward the second property on Main. "Of course, this one is only a few doors from the building you bought a few weeks ago."

"I'd like to get Madison's opinion, but I'll let you know soon."

"And Dr. Collins, I'm surprised as well as pleased you shared your information with me." She patted him on the shoulder. "We need another doctor in Cranberry Cove. Did you know that Dr. Murray is retiring soon? Your timing is impeccable."

God's timing. "No." He smiled.

Janette offered her hand once more. "I'll wait for your phone call."

"Likely tomorrow." Micah headed toward his car parked on the next block. He neared the local jewelry shop and stopped to peer inside. Wedding rings lined the window, sparkling in the sun. Movement behind him caught his eyes.

Without turning, he lifted his gaze. Between two buildings, at the opening of the alley, Ford stood staring in his direction.

Leaving the blossoming hope of a future with a woman he was coming to love, Micah paced toward his car. When he reached the driver's door, he turned to look.

Mr. Ford had gone.

Micah took the frozen meal out of the freezer. Chicken, mashed potatoes, and corn. Not exactly like his mother used to make. If he had his choice, he'd rather share a meal with Madison tonight. Someday … they would spend every leisurely hour together, every evening and every night.

A tap on the door brought him back from his dreams. Maybe a neighbor wanting to borrow something—or one of those groups asking him to go to their church. Micah looked through the peep hole and groaned.

Victoria stood on his sidewalk, shifting from one foot to the other.

He opened the door. "How did you know my address?"

Dark circles marred her eyes. "I looked it up. May I come in?" Her long hair she usually curled lay straight on her shoulders. She wasn't wearing as much makeup.

"I'm not sure that it's a good idea, Victoria. Your behavior at the store was a little unsettling. We had this conversation before. You could hurt someone with those outbursts."

"Micah, I've driven here from the inn. The least you could do is to let me come inside. I'll only take a minute."

Against his better judgment, he opened the door.

She glanced around at his living room, probably surprised at his small quarters. "Your apartment is quite a change from your house in Sacramento."

"I can't afford anything too extravagant on a store manager's pay."

She whirled around to face him. "Why, Micah? Why

did you come here? Was it really to forget about Ellen so we could have a life together?"

Micah gulped and widened his eyes. He looked around the apartment to see if any valuables were laying around. "Victoria, I will never forget Ellen. She was and will always be an important part of my life." When she didn't move to destroy his home, he rubbed his head and pointed to his couch for her to sit down. "And as I informed you in the store, I have never entertained thoughts of you and me in any capacity outside my practice and my treatment of you as a patient."

"If you didn't want to forget about Ellen, why did you run so far?"

Seemed to Micah she was picking and choosing what she wanted to hear from him.

"I don't believe that this is a conversation you and I are meant to have. You were my patient. I'm not practicing right now, and though you seem to believe that there was more between us than there was, nothing will ever happen between us."

"I believe part of you misses me. As soon as your heart has fully healed from your loss, I think you'll realize the truth. I need for you to know, I'm here when that day comes." She smoothed her hand over his.

Micah slowly moved his hand from her touch. "Victoria—"

She placed her finger on his lips. "No, don't say anything now. Wait. You'll know when the time is right." She turned to him and threw her arms around his neck. "One day … "

How could he discourage her if she wasn't willing to listen? He moved away from her and stood. "The neighbors are going to accuse me of being a womanizer if any more attractive blonds show up."

"Blonds? You're talking about that Madison, aren't you?"

"Again, not a conversation for us based on our lack of relationship."

She clenched her hands, but as if thinking second thoughts, she released them and followed him to the door, which he held open for her. She blinked wet eyelashes and grasped his hand. "Bye for now, Micah."

"Care to answer a question for me?"

"If I can, based on our relationship and all ..." She swayed seductively.

"Did Bates tell you to come to Cranberry Cove?"

Her body swaying, she shook her head. "He told me where you are, and he explained how it is between you and me—you know, Ellen and all—and I decided to come on my own. I'm not here with Bates." She touched his hair hanging over his forehead. "You know, I dated his son, Liam, for a while. He never compared to you." Her face softened, and sorrow filled her eyes.

"Good night, Victoria. Please be careful going home."

Micah slowly closed the door and stepped back into the living room. No doubt, Victoria brought emotional baggage with her to his apartment. She had never been taught to cope with loss or disappointment, that was obvious. She remained tense and conflicted. He hated to see the pain in her eyes when she left, but he couldn't tell her what she wanted to hear.

Micah moseyed into the kitchen again and popped the meal in the microwave. He bowed his head. "Lord, only You can meet her needs. Please heal her heart."

He pulled out his phone when the text signal dinged.

Come to the inn tomorrow evening. We're having a dinner featuring French cuisine. MM.

Now that girl, he could tell everything about his life, and someday, he would.

Chapter Twenty-Five

Bates relaxed onto the chaise lounge in front of his cabin. He slipped on a pair of sunglasses, closed his eyes, and lifted his face to the sun. Glorious. Southern Washington had a lot to offer him. Perhaps he'd relocate here. No. He needed to return home soon and see about his construction company. Liam couldn't manage it alone forever.

A motor hummed and stopped.

Bates sat up and whipped off his sunglasses.

Victoria stepped out of her Porsche and marched toward him.

By her furrowed brows, he figured this wasn't a social call. He cleared his throat, stood, and pulled up a lawn chair. "Good morning, my dear. Sit and enjoy the sun with me."

She nodded and slipped into the Adirondack patio chair.

Her heavy sigh told him she harbored concerns. Dr. Collins, no doubt. "Would you like a cup of coffee?"

"No, thank you. I had some at the inn." Victoria crossed her ankles. "When we first spoke about my presence in Cranberry Cove, you said Micah needed me, that underneath his pain, he cared for me. That's not what he's telling me."

"Well, don't concern yourself with what he says. He's trying to discover his purpose after the death of his wife. Where he wants to go from here." He fiddled with his fingers. "When you see him, have you asked him about his life after his wife's death? Or have you simply declared your unending devotion?"

She moved her head as if he'd slapped her. "Are you saying that I'm self-centered, Mr. Bates?"

"No, not at all. Tell me, then, what does he say about his plans?"

She bounded to her feet. "You're awful. You got me in to this. I could have gone on, gotten over him, but here I am …"

"Here you are …?" Bates waved his hand. "Doing what?"

She stomped her foot. "Listening to a foolish old man who doesn't care anything about me. She bent downward and into his face. "What are you up to, Mr. Bates? Are you really here to seek forgiveness? Didn't you get it? Isn't it time to leave now?"

Bates measured his breaths. If she wasn't careful, he'd teach her a lesson about respect.

"Truthfully," she said, "I'm ready to go home. From the rumors that circulate around the inn, Micah is involved with Madison Mitchell. She works at the inn. She's a janitor. What does he see in her, anyway?"

"I don't know because you're much more beautiful than she. Look, Victoria, your best move now is to get to know the opponent. Approach her. Make friends. Spy on the enemy camp."

She marched toward the door, her heels pecking the

wood flooring.

"So?" He caught up to her at the edge of the porch.

She waved her hand in the air. "Good-bye, Mr. Bates. Tell Liam hello for me."

Bates went back inside the cabin.

Victoria wasn't proving as useful as he'd thought she'd be.

Madison's heart pattered a little harder at the knock. She threw the studio door open and grinned at Micah. "Glad you could make it."

"I couldn't turn down an invitation to eat at the inn." He laughed.

"I'm sorry I couldn't join you to look at the properties Monday. Ashton sent me to Oceanview to purchase some ingredients for the dinner tonight. Tony's making one of Juliette's favorite French recipes."

"Speaking of our former chef, has anyone heard from her and Ryder?"

"Ashton said she got an e-mail. Ryder's almost fluent in French and running the hotel on his own—and Juliette's father retired. She has morning sickness and is at home half the time. She can't stand the smell of certain food when they're cooking."

"That will pass soon." Micah smiled. "Happy for them. Ryder talked a lot about being a dad one day." He sniffed the air. "Speaking of food. What do I smell? I'm starved."

They stepped out of the studio, and Madison locked the door. "Did you find a location for your practice?"

"Two. I snapped a few shots and want your opinion."

"Be glad to. Can you survive without food long enough to take a look at my latest creation?"

"In your studio?"

"No. I'll show you."

He gave her a smile that said what mattered to her mattered to him. "Sure."

Madison grasped Micah's hand and led him to the spot near Aunt Gina's grave where she and Ashton had hammered the wrought iron base into the ground. The rectangular, stained-glass creation hung from a garden flag holder. "Besides my suncatcher which was smashed to bits, this is my first major accomplishment."

Underneath the tree only a few feet from the grave maker, the blues, golds, and browns featured a cross in the middle with rays shooting outward to the perimeter.

Micah kneeled and ran his finger over the glass sections. "What's the significance?"

Madison dropped beside him. "The design represents the cross of Jesus in the center of one's life, and the rays are the times when Christians share the message with others."

"So, you placed it near Gina's grave to make a statement?"

"Yes, Ashton's told many stories about her. Aunt Gina demonstrated a life of giving and service to the Lord." Madison stood again. "I only met her once when Ashton and I were in college. We came to the inn to visit for spring break. I knew there was something different about her, but I was too stubborn to understand."

He rose and smiled. "Well, not anymore."

Something lying on the ground close to the tree caught her attention. "What's this?" She reached to pick up the item and turned over a pen in her hands. "Looks like someone dropped this. The writing on the side says Ford's Detective Services of Sacramento. Guess we know who lost it."

Micah frowned and reached for the pen. "So, at least that much is true. Mind if I keep this? It might come in handy."

Madison shrugged. "Do you think you might need a detective?"

"No." He grinned. "I'm thinking I might need the phone number of a prying individual who's one step away from having charges filed against him for stalking."

Chapter Twenty-Six

Madison cleared the lunch dishes from the dining room tables and rolled the utility cart into the kitchen.

The parttime college student who worked on weekends glanced her way and smiled. "I'll take those."

Ashton walked into the kitchen and glanced at Madison. "Would you mind dusting the living room and hall this afternoon?"

"Of course. Be happy to." With her use of Ashton's studio, doing extra chores was the least she could do for her friend.

"I don't know what's going to happen when you start back to school this fall."

Madison gathered her dusting cloth, wood cleaner, and feather duster. "You'll find somebody. Merely working in this gorgeous old inn is payment enough." She headed toward the living room.

A light coat of dust covered the elegant maple coffee table. Madison ran her cloth over the surface until she saw a shine. Smiling, she turned to the side table.

"Hello, Madison. Taking good care of this beautiful antique furniture, I see."

Madison straightened and turned toward the person speaking. Victoria. *Be nice.* "Well, hello to you, too. Are you enjoying your stay in Cranberry Cove?"

"Yes, and I'll never forget this wonderful old inn." Victoria relaxed into one of the side chairs. "Have you worked here long?"

"No, only since June. I'm helping Ashton for the summer." Madison set the bottle of oil on the side table and took a chair adjacent to Victoria. Unsure if this was the best move, she'd only sit a couple of minutes. But Victoria seemed genuinely interested in starting up a conversation. Ashton always said that guests came first.

"So, what do you do for the rest of the year?" Victoria peered at her as if she really wanted to hear the answer.

"I'm a high school teacher in Cranberry Cove."

Victoria stared, as if she didn't believe her. "That's an important job. Kids are so awkward at that age. At least I was."

"You're such an attractive lady today that I can't imagine you were."

Victoria's face reddened as if no one had ever paid her a compliment. She crossed one leg and then uncrossed it. "Are you from around here?"

Madison scratched her head. Victoria was merely acting friendly, right? She cleared her throat. "Actually, I grew up in Port Orchard. What about you?"

"I was born and raised in Sacramento." Her gaze darted from one part of the room to another, clearly uncomfortable with the conversation she'd initiated. "Dr. Collins is wonderful, isn't he?"

Madison smiled. "Very. Isn't it great that he's going back into practice?"

"Micah's going back to Sacramento?" Victoria's

mood lightened, and she nearly bounded in her chair.

Madison shook her head. "He's going to open a practice here where he's also opening up a cancer care center. Isn't that exciting?"

Victoria stood, seeming to restrain some type of rage. "I supposed so. I suppose also that you're the reason he's staying here."

"Not necessarily. I've only known Micah a short time. I believe he likes the area and the people here. He feels as if he's home."

"I see." Victoria lifted her lilt nose and walked away, back stiff, head held high.

Madison watched through the front windows until Victoria backed out her car from the parking lot and drove away.

Madison shook her head. Strange. For a while, she'd assumed the woman wanted to make friendly conversation. Now she wasn't too sure. So, what were her intentions?

Chapter Twenty-Seven

Micah opened the car door for Madison, and they stepped toward Janette at the front of his potential medical office.

Madison gave a thumbs up. "A downtown office is a wise move."

Janette stuck her key in the lock, and he and Madison walked in behind her.

Janette pointed down the hall. "There're several spaces which could serve as exam rooms or your office, Micah." She grinned at him. "I'm still getting use to the idea that you're Dr. Micah Collins."

Micah smiled. "I'm happy to assume my former profession, helping people with health issues. One major difference is, I'll have men as well as women patients. Haven't treated men since I was doing my residency."

Madison wrapped her arm around his. "You'll be a good doctor, too. I'm proud of you."

Janette paused in the larger room to the right. "This will make a good reception room, and it's adjacent to the potential examination rooms."

He looked at Madison. "So, you agree, a downtown location works well as opposed to one on the edge of town or closer to the inn?"

She nodded. "Don't forget, you're only a couple of doors away from The Caring Center. You can head over right after work."

He snickered. "I don't even get a dinner break?"

Madison stood on tiptoes and kissed his cheek. "I'll consider it."

"Okay, I'm sold. Janette, I'd like to make an offer on the property before someone takes it off the market."

"Well, let's go to my office right now." She smiled.

On the way to the realty office, Madison grinned. "I know I said this before, but I am so proud of you."

They walked along together, Janette in front of them. "This will be different from Sacramento, a smaller, more personal practice."

Madison grimaced.

"What's that about?" he asked.

"Don't make it too personal. I spoke with Victoria yesterday. She really is attracted to you, Dr. Collins, and when I told her you might have plans to stay here in Cranberry Cove, she was none-too-happy." She pretended to swipe her brow with the back of her hand. "She can be intense."

Micah stopped and tugged Madison to a halt. "Avoid her, okay? I don't want anything happening to you. What you said to her could have set her off yesterday. If she pushed you or harmed you in any way ..."

Madison hugged him, and Micah accepted the warm and comfort. "I'll be on my guard. I promise."

Monday after work, Madison relaxed in the inn's living room for a moment after cleaning the rooms. She opened the small Bible Micah had offered when she first prayed with him.

"Hello, Miss Mitchell."

Madison glanced up at the familiar voice. "Micah."

He edged down beside her. "I decided we've had enough stress for a while. I'm taking you on a surprise outing."

"Where are we going?"

"It wouldn't be a surprise if I told you." Micah stood and gave her a hand up. "Trust me. You'll have fun. We're driving about thirty miles out of town. We've got plenty of daylight, and I promise. You'll love it."

"Perfect timing. I'm finished with work for today." To take a break from cleaning for a while sounded wonderful. "Do I need to change?"

"No. You look gorgeous as you are. Even jeans and a shirt look dressy on you." He kissed her cheek.

In Micah's car, they traveled west toward the wharf and turned north out of town on the road that lined the bay.

"In a few more miles, you have to close your eyes and cover them with your hands. And no peeking."

"Dr. Collins, what are you up to?"

He glanced from the road, winked at her, and turned his attention to the tree-lined route up the coast. "Okay, time to close your eyes."

Madison complied. "No peeking, I promise." She couldn't see, but she could smell the ocean salt air mixed and a hint of evergreen trees.

Micah slowed the car and turned to the right. "You're not peeking?"

"Nope, I promise." She took in another long breath. A new scent wafted through the open window. Flowers? A sweet and herbal smell. "Micah, where are we?"

Micah slowed the car and stopped. "Sit still and don't look. I'll come around the other side to get you."

Tempted to peek, Madison squeezed her eyes tighter. She wouldn't spoil Micah's surprise. Her passenger door opened.

"Here's my hand." His warm fingers grasped hers as she stepped out of the car, still keeping her eyes shut. "This way."

Now the strong, delicate, floral yet woodsy scent gave her a clue. "My nose figured it out. I smell lavender. We're at a lavender farm."

He led her about thirty steps along a path which felt like pebbles under her feet and stopped. "Okay, open your eyes."

Madison caught her breath. Fields and fields of aromatic lavender plants swayed in the breeze. Long, straight rows of the bushes were perfectly aligned to create mounds of gray and lavender blue.

"You guessed it. This is McNary's Lavender Farm."

Madison filled her lungs with another delightful breath of the aroma. "The fields look like purple waves on the sea." She pointed to an ornate bench across from the field. "Let's go over there. I want to snap some pictures."

All thoughts of any danger in Cranberry Cove seemed to evaporate. Madison lifted her phone for a couple of shots to remind her of the gorgeous day. She turned to kiss his prickly cheek. "I don't ever want to leave." Resting her head on Micah's shoulder felt right.

Later, Micah smiled and stood. "There's a gift shop

if you'd like to check it out."

Inside the shop, Madison selected a tin of lavender tea, a bag of potpourri, and several bars of lavender soap. "Ashton would love this." Madison paid for the items and hooked the sack on her arm.

At Micah's car, she stopped and turned to him. "I loved today."

Micah leaned nearer and swept a strand of hair off her neck. "Very soon, I want to talk about our future—together."

His lips brushed hers, his woody scent dizzying. The soft tickle of his breath raced her pulse, and she slipped her arms around his shoulders. Yes, she was ready—to discuss a life with Micah.

Micah pulled up in front of the inn. The well-lit entrance beckoned, reminding him of home. Someday, he wanted a home—one with Madison.

"My car is around by the kitchen entrance if you don't mind dropping me off there." Madison gathered her purse. As he turned the corner, Madison pointed. "Right there by Ashton's car. I can't believe she's still here."

"I'm sure she's just stopped by." Gravel crunched under his tires as Micah took the road leading to the other entrance. He crept past the garbage bin and stopped at the side door. He sensed movement and glanced into his rearview mirror.

Car lights shone and then dimmed as someone pulled up from the main road into the parking lot. A guest checking in?

Micah moved the car as close as he could to the side entrance under a fir growing near the unlit area. Rushing around to Madison's door, he grasped her elbow. "Someone may be following us."

Madison clutched his arm tight and drew in a long breath.

The sound of footsteps clomped behind them.

"Go inside. Hurry." Micah turned in the direction of the sound.

A man barely visible in the moonless night took slow strides toward him. "Dr. Collins?"

Micah went on high alert. This wasn't Ford or even Bates.

Madison's arm on his shoulder told him she hadn't done as he requested. "Be careful," she whispered.

The tall guy with broad shoulders in a wide-brimmed hat sitting low on his forehead stepped out of the shadows and lifted both hands. "Can we talk?"

Micah fingered the gun he'd decided to carry. "If you'll step inside through the front entrance, my date and I will join you in a moment."

The man hesitated but then nodded and looked behind him. "Listen, I have to go, but I'm here to warn you that—"

Micah pounced forward. "Not another warning. Who are you? What do you really want?"

"The man opened his car door and ducked inside. "Just be careful, you and your girl." He slammed the door and squealed out of sight.

"I don't know what to think." Micah turned and gripped his hair in his hands. "I have always lived a peaceful existence if you take away a dying wife and a lawsuit for malpractice. I can't begin to understand what in the world is going on here."

Madison touched his arm. "We need to go inside?"

"Now? Why? I thought I'd follow you home."

"Because the last thing that man wanted to do was enter the inn. That must mean that whoever he's warning you against is inside."

Micah nodded. "You're very smart. Has anyone ever told you that?"

"Yes, an incredibly handsome doctor just did."

Micah led her around to the front of the inn and opened the door for her.

"Micah!" Victoria stood from a chair in the living area but stopped and sat down when she saw Madison.

"Just the man I wanted to see." Bates came from the dining area. "Any chance your schedule has given you a break to have our fishing lesson tomorrow?"

Micah looked between Bates and Victoria and back to Madison.

Madison gave an imperceptible nod.

Micah followed the direction, up the stairs. His gaze met Mr. Ford's.

The detective mouthed the words. "Listen…"

Micah shook his head at the meaning he didn't quite comprehend.

"So …" Bates pestered. "Tomorrow, any time. You, too, ma'am. Join us."

"There are three possibilities," Madison whispered.

"Pardon?" Bates asked, his voice loud. "What did you say?"

"Nothing," Madison answered. "I'd love you join you any time you do the lesson."

Micah pulled out his phone to check his calendar to appear polite. "I'm sorry. Once I have the center open, I'll

make your lesson a priority."
Anything to get one suspect out of his hair.

Chapter Twenty-Eight

The next evening, Madison plopped down on her comfortable bed in her apartment and glanced out the window. The sun approached the horizon, and the trees behind the complex grew long. With her doors securely locked this evening, she felt safe from whoever had intentions of harming her and Micah. She prayed nothing would come of either of the men's warnings.

Her pulse stilled, and she allowed herself to imagine her future. She could almost picture her gorgeous husband by her side as they strolled along Cranberry Cove's Bay. Bright sun shone as they listened to the seagulls' squawks and croons. Micah leaned toward her with a kiss that stole the breath in her lungs. The handsome doctor was hers for as long as the Lord allowed—

Her phone's usual jingle played, intruding on her revery. She reached for her cell lying on the bed beside her.

"Madison, this is Lorelei, the co-owner of Gianna's studio. I haven't been in lately as I'm preparing to retire."

"Yes, Lorelei. I remember seeing you the first night I started lessons. Your work is beautiful."

"Thank you, but it's time for me to retire. My husband and I are selling our house and traveling in our RV. I love the craft of creating stained-glass art, but it's time for us to set sail and see the United States."

"That sounds wonderful." If she and Micah were married and had an RV, she might want to do the same. At least she wouldn't have to worry about medical care on the road. She'd have her own doctor by her side. She chuckled at the silly thoughts.

"You're probably wondering why I'm calling. I'm selling my entire collection of supplies, tools, and glass. Gianna has spoken highly of your abilities, and I'd like to offer you the opportunity to purchase my equipment at a reduced price before I advertise online. If you're interested.

Lorelei quoted a price, and Madison's chin fell to her chest. "It's a wonderful offer. I'd have to finance the equipment, but if I taught school one more year, I could pay it off." Then, God willing, she could open her own studio.

"Let's talk soon."

Madison closed her eyes once more. She'd received an opportunity to purchase needed equipment to open a studio. And best of all, she'd come to know the Lord when the handsome doctor she'd fallen for had shared the gospel with her. Her life had made a turn—for the best. Men with binoculars, others in fishing gear. Even the guy who claimed to be unarmed. They all seemed to fade from her thoughts. How could anything go wrong now?

Micah opened the meeting with prayer and then glanced around the circle of people. Mrs. Caldwell, the woman who came into the shop that day looking at fishing vests, was there. Mr. and Mrs. Whitlock who heard about the group from Pastor Ethridge at Cove Community Church sat next to her. Madison sat by his side, and finally, Karina, a scarf covering her head, was next to her husband. He'd left word at the inn for Victoria, hoping she'd join them, but the troubled woman had not shown. He hadn't had an opportunity to tell Bates about the inaugural meeting.

"Thank you all for coming to the very first Caring Center activity. We'll go around the circle and introduce ourselves."

The turnout was more than Micah could've hoped for. When his turn came around, he smiled at Madison. "I couldn't have opened The Caring Center without my friend Madison Mitchell and, of course, Pastor Ethridge who secured funds to pay for the building." He squeezed Madison's hand and nodded to the pastor. "Thank you. And to all of you. I pray you'll find fellowship and healing through our Lord, Jesus Christ. You will not face your battle alone."

The event, complete with punch and cake and a time of fellowship went smoothly with participants making counseling appointments and signing up for other events. Each of those seeking help indicated they'd made friends on their journey that would benefit from the center, and they vowed to tell them.

Micah and Madison made sure the center was clean and ready for the next day before they left. Madison took kitchen duty, and Micah did cleanup, stepping outside in the alley to toss the trash.

Something scampered nearby the dumpster, and Micah jumped. Then he laughed as a cat meowed and skirted across the street.

He headed back inside but stopped, sure that he'd heard footsteps. "Hello?"

No one responded.

He shrugged and stepped inside, locking the door.

"All done." Madison met him in the front room.

They stepped out onto the walkway in front of the storefront. Micah stared up at the sky. Even downtown, the stars shone brightly.

Beside him, Madison looked up and then turned her head to face him.

Micah couldn't resist. He lowered his lips to hers, taking her in his arms and hugging her tightly. Lost in her warm embrace, he could have stayed there forever.

Crash.

Madison jerked away from him and squealed in panic as glass shattered around them.

A bottle lay busted on the ground.

"It barely missed us." Madison's attention darted around them. "That wasn't an accident."

"Let's get inside," Micah opened the door again and pushed Madison inside. "Did you see anyone?"

"No. It came out of nowhere."

Micah tugged her away from the glass door and windows and turned on the light. "The front window is up to code or it sure would have shattered. It would have come right down on us." He shivered. "Are you sure— you're bleeding." He touched her forehead. "Did the bottle hit you?"

"I—I don't think so." She brushed her hand over the

cut. Blood graced her fingers. "Maybe a shard hit me when it hit the glass."

"This isn't something we can—"

Madison gripped his arm. "I smell smoke."

In the kitchen, smoke filtered in through the cracks in the door. Micah felt the door and came away from it quick. "We can't open it." He tugged her with him to the front. "Wait here by the door, but don't go outside."

"Where are you going?"

"I'm going to try to save the block." He rushed outside and down the alley.

A fire blazed up the back door to the center. Someone had set boxes from the dumpster on fire.

Micah whipped out his phone and called 9-1-1 and searched for any source of water.

A tap between the dry cleaners next door and the center caught his attention. A small hose had been left attached. He turned the knob and prayed it worked.

Water sputtered out, and Micah sprayed the fire and up into the rafter where it had started to catch. If it had gotten any higher … or near the chemicals that dry cleaners used … He didn't want to think about it. Sirens split the air.

Madison ran around the corner and stopped. She placed her hand over her mouth. "This wasn't an accident either."

"You're right."

Trouble was, he had been certain he knew who threw the bottle, but the fire changed his assumptions.

Victoria had an impulsive temper, but she wasn't one to build a fire.

Chapter Twenty-Nine

Six days after the fire, the damage to the center repaired, Micah reached for his ringing phone. The county sheriff's number appeared on the screen. He headed for his office and signaled for Karina to take care of the front. "Micah Collins, how can I help you?"

"Mr. Collins. Sheriff Clayborn. I received a report from the fire chief, and I thought I'd give you a call."

"Yes, sir."

"While we knew the fire was intentionally set, the arson investigators could not locate a single surveillance camera in the area to see who entered and left the scene. And as it turns out, we have no witnesses. I'm sorry, but short of a confession, it's not likely that we'll catch our culprit."

"Is your department closing the investigation?"

"One of our detectives has been assigned the case and will do some additional follow up. Not likely and impossible aren't the same. I only wanted you to know that we aren't close to catching anyone. Both the thrown bottle and the fire seem to indicate that either you or Ms. Mitchell or both were targets."

Micah hung up from the call. He hadn't mentioned

Victoria to the responding officers. Now, he wished he had.

Bates slammed his hands in his pocket and walked into the grand entrance to the inn. Victoria wanted to meet him in the chapel. She wanted to talk. Ha. What did she want to complain about this time?

He scrunched his brows. He'd begun to believe he'd made a mistake coaxing her to accompany him to Cranberry Cove. She'd proven herself to be a huge liability. He supposed he'd overestimated her charm with Collins.

He turned the corner and walked down the main hall. As he'd recalled, the old chapel sat to the right. First chapel he'd frequented in many a year.

Through the double wooden doors, Bates could see Victoria down front on the first row. Ugh. Why'd she have to sit all the way down there. "Victoria?" He set out toward the large altar and stained-glass window.

She turned to face him when he slipped down beside her. "Mr. Bates, I can't do this anymore." She covered her face, and her shoulders shook.

What a child. He should've known she was weak. "What seems to be the problem, my dear?"

She mopped her face and hiccupped at couple of times. "I can't pretend that Micah feels anything for me other than as he would for any other patient. I—I get so angry, and ..." She cried into her hands. "I do things ..."

Bates straightened. "What kind of things, Victoria?"

She shook her head. "I'm going home. I wanted to

meet you so you'd know. I'd like you to tell Micah I'm sorry."

Bates squirmed on the wooden bench. How did people sit here for an hour? "What are you sorry for?" he pressed.

"Please just tell him that I'm sorry."

Bates forced back the smile that threatened. She wasn't going to be a liability at all. "I'll tell him."

She sniffed and dabbed her nose. "I'm going to drive home."

"Time to think. That's good. I'm sure wonderful things await you when you return, but are you sure you're up to the drive."

"If she's not, I'll drive her."

Bates stood at the sound of his son's voice. "Liam, what are you doing here?"

"Never mind that. We're not going to be here for long. Victoria, why don't you pack and join me and Dad. We're going home."

Victoria widened her eyes and nodded. "You came here for me?"

"I came here for you both. You've been gone long enough. Haven't you done enough, Dad?"

Victoria stopped sniveling and stared at Liam.

Bates took a deep breath. "Not long enough," he countered his son.

"Dad, I know what you're up to, and I want it to stop."

"Stop what?" Bates growled. "I've done nothing."

"Stop it!" Liam came forward, grasping Bates's arms. "What about me? She was my mother, you know. Did you ever think about that?"

Bates gripped his fist into a tight ball, ready to punch Liam in the head. The boy was interfering, keeping him from doing what he had to do. "Yes, of course, I understand."

Liam released Bates and patted Victoria's back, and once again her shoulders shook. He lowered his voice. "I haven't seen you for a while. Is there anything I can do to help you get ready to leave?"

Bates gritted his teeth. Through it all, he'd prided himself on keeping his anger in check, on presenting the face everyone had wanted to see through all he'd endured. Lately, he struggled to keep the rage contained. "How did you know where to find me?"

"I have my ways, and I know everything you've done and most likely plan to do." Liam put his arm around Bates's shoulder. "I love you, you know. You're all I've got."

Victoria hiccupped and covered her mouth. "You have me, too, Mr. Bates."

That's all he needed. A sniveling son and a spoiled princess. Life couldn't get much better.

Unless he made it that way.

In the inn's entry, Micah clutched Madison's hand. "I thought it best to talk to you in person about what the sheriff had to say about the fire. You'll never believe it. Shall we talk privately? Perhaps in the chapel?"

Madison grasped his arm to restrain him. "I saw some others go in there a while ago. In fact, I believe I saw Victoria and Mr. Bates go through the front door. We can peek in and see if they're still in there."

Micah stopped at the chapel, the door sitting open.

Victoria walked up the aisle toward them followed by Bates and another man who had his arms around the old guy's shoulders. Micah swallowed hard. He knew that guy. He was the man who'd approached him and Madison when they returned from the lavender farm.

Bates's face lit when he saw Micah and Madison. "Hello. Nice to see you." He stepped out of the reach of the other man. "Have you met my son, Liam?"

Madison squeezed Micah's hand harder and gulped.

Liam stepped in front of Bates and shook Micah's hand. "Yes, we met the other night at the inn. I had, er, stopped by to talk to Victoria and ran into them." The guy cast a quick glance to his father and back to Micah before giving an almost imperceptible shake of his head.

Micah firmed his lips and backed away. "She said you'd dated. Are you here to win her back?"

"Something like that," the younger Bates said.

Jax Bates patted Micah's shoulder. "Wouldn't that be a fine match?"

Micah faltered over a response. A strong man would eventually cower to that girl's tantrums.

"We're heading back. Tonight," the son advised. "You won't have to worry about us."

Micah caught the meaning, but he didn't know to whom the reference was made.

"Right, Dad?" Liam seemed to bait his father.

"Yeah, right," Bates grumbled.

Chapter Thirty

Sunday after church, Micah carried the picnic basket, and Madison hauled the fishing equipment.

Today, he wanted to replicate an important day in their lives. Micah suspected he'd fallen in love with Madison before the day they came here to the stream to fish. If he admitted it, he was sure he'd fallen for her when he saw her face after she'd thrown the rod at him in the store.

What better way to commemorate?

Victoria and Bates were well out of town, back in Sacramento with Bates's son, Liam, and though he hadn't checked out of his room at the inn, Mr. Ford had kept to himself.

The sun was high in the sky when Micah placed the heavy picnic box on the ground and hurried to take Madison's load.

He slipped his fingers around Madison's hand. "Thank you for humoring me and coming out here. As far as I'm concerned, this is our spot. I'll never bring another customer out here for a lesson."

She laughed. "You better not, especially one of the feminine persuasion."

"This is just the place to allow God's peace to wash over us." Despite all else, the Lord had a future for them. "When we have everything in order, the new practice, the center, I want to talk about what comes next for us." He paused, gazing into her beautiful eyes the color of the sky on a summer morning.

She glanced up at him and smiled, one that said *I want to be with you always.*

"I love you, Madison Mitchell." He held her close, her body so near his he could sense the thumping of her heart.

She tiptoed and kissed his cheek. "I've come to realize, you're the only man I've really loved."

Micah trailed his lips along her chin line and then touched her lips with his. Now he knew nothing but the warmth of the afternoon sun, the breeze from the waters of the stream, and Madison.

Deep into a kiss, Madison broke away. "Uhm…" she murmured. "We're being watched."

Micah closed his eyes. "Ford, again?"

"No. I don't think so, but it's a man. He's on the ridge."

Micah turned.

"He's gone." Madison sighed. "Maybe he was another fisherman." She patted his cheek playfully. "He did save us, though." Her cheeks reddened. "Dr. Collins, you kiss in such a way that it curls a woman's toes."

He laughed aloud. "Just wait. You just wait, Madison Mitchell…"

"Well, well, looks like I'm interrupting a tender moment." The man's words accompanied his crashing through the thicket.

Micah stepped away from Madison, grasped her

hand, and peered in the direction of the voice. "Bates. Did you come all the way back to Cranberry Cove for a fishing lesson?"

Bates took a few steps toward them, one hand in his pocket. "Not exactly, but I see that you had no problem scheduling one without me. How'd you know, Micah?"

Micah frowned. "How did I know what? He didn't like the tone the man used, and the usual lightness was gone in the man's stance. This was a different Bates than the one who'd gone home with his son.

Micah turned away, reaching for his rod. "You can join us." He lifted the equipment toward Bates.

"Micah," Madison hissed.

Micah straightened and brought the rod back toward him.

The man held a gun on Madison. "I've waited for this moment ever since Mary died."

A cloak of dark, cloying fear wrapped around Micah. "Bates, what are you talking about?" He pushed Madison away from Bates and behind him.

"You thought you'd won—that I simply let your offense go unpunished."

The high screech of a seagull made Micah jump. "If you'll recall, you accepted the settlement. Bates, I wasn't to blame for the embolism your wife died from. It could've happened anytime in her life."

"They paid!" Bates screeched. "They paid me. That meant they knew. They knew all along, and they saved your career. I lost my wife, and you lost nothing."

"Mr. Bates, insurance companies settle to avoid other payouts. My account was one of thousands with them. They have to cut their losses. Trials, whether you win or lose them, cost money and resources. And they probably kept you from paying my attorney's fees."

"What are you talking about? Me pay your fees? I sued you."

"If I had won the suit, the insurance company would have filed a Motion for Attorney's Fees. They always do. When I agreed to settle, I didn't want you to face that possibility. We'd both lost so much already. If the jury had ruled in your favor, I would have had insurance coverage, but you had nothing but your business to fall back upon. I couldn't have you lose that to pay for fees."

"No." Bates mumbled. He pointed the gun in the air and fired. Once. Twice. A third time. "Noooo." He screamed.

He brought the gun down, leveling it at Micah.

Madison hugged him from behind.

Bates scowled. "You have your sweet little lady by your side." He yelled. "Where's mine, I ask you? I would rather have lost everything … I'd have taken the chance. I wasn't going to lose. You killed my wife."

"Mr. Bates," Micah calmed his voice, "where's your son?"

Bates blinked and seemed lost for a moment. Then he shook his head. "He's moved on, too. He took me home and left me there while he and Victoria …" The man lowered his head and shook it fiercely.

Liam had been trying to warn them. Bates was a disturbed man, broken by his wife's death. "Your son is going to be worried," Micah reasoned. "I'm worried about you, too. Let me get you some help."

"I'm sick and tired of playing games with you." Bates's hand shook as he fingered the trigger. "I tried to burn down your little center, but she stopped me." He blinked several times.

"Who? Who stopped you?"

"Victoria. She came out of nowhere. The blaze would've burned hot. You would have never put it out."

"You threw the bottle at us," Madison accused.

"What bottle?" Bates seemed confused. "Why would I throw a bottle at you. I want him hurting, lacking the things he took from me." He snarled. "I want him dead, not wounded, and right now, I have the opportunity to do both."

Micah had to act or Bates would kill him and then turn the gun on Madison. He whipped the rod in the air and struck at the older man.

Bates stumbled but still held the gun on Micah.

"No!" Madison rushed toward Bates and shoved him with her two hands.

Bates stumbled but turned toward her. "You little …" He swung out, hitting Madison on the side of the head with the gun's nose.

Madison groaned and slipped onto the sand, eyes closed.

Fury exploded in Micah, and he lunged toward Bates. "She's an innocent woman. How dare you?"

"That's it." Bates raised his gun and fired.

A bullet whizzed over Micah's shoulder. He stumbled on a rock and toppled onto the ground.

Bates slowly walked closer and stood over Micah, pointing the gun at his head. "I'm taking a better aim this time."

Micah lifted to his knees. He couldn't let an insane man win. A kick to the face sent Micah down again.

Once more, Bates aimed. "You better pray that God of yours has mercy on you because you're going to see Him soon."

Micah groaned. "Dear Lord, please protect Madison if this is the end for me."

"Jackson Bates!" a man, his voice sounding like thunder, spoke from somewhere nearby.

Bates stumbled back, the gun swinging in the air. "God?"

Madison raised up and pointed something in Bates's face.

The man screamed in pain and fell to the ground, covering his eyes with his hand.

Micah lunged forward and took the gun from him. He stepped back and pointed the weapon at their assailant. "What was that?"

"Oh, just bear spray. It's about three times as potent as pepper spray. Since this all started, I've kept it in my pocket all the time."

Micah laughed in pure relief. "I was afraid Bates had hurt you."

Madison did a complete turnaround. "Someone spoke and caught his attention. Right after you prayed. Didn't you hear?"

A crashing came through the woods, and a man emerged.

"My eyes!" Bates squirmed. "Help me."

Micah lifted his gun at Ford.

"Now, Micah, haven't you figured it all out yet." Ford didn't stop. He made his way to Bates, picked him up and carried him to the stream where he dumped him in and left him submerged a moment. When he pulled Bates up, the man flailed. Ford stuffed him under again. "Better, Mr. Bates? The water is good for your eyes. Now, shut up or I'll shut you up." He reached behind him and pulled out a zip tie. "No one was hurt here, right?" He shook

Bates.

"By the grace of God," Madison choked out.

"By the grace of God," Ford repeated. "He is a mighty God, isn't He? Put the gun down, Micah, and let me tell you a little story."

Micah kept the gun in place. "Tell me the story first."

"A worried son who found a mutilated picture of a doctor who'd recently operated on his mother who was lost on the surgical table, hired a detective to follow his deeply distraught old man and protect him and the doctor who'd operated on his wife. When the detective followed him to a little hole in the wall in Washington, he found that he no longer had only one person to follow, but two, who might bring harm to the doctor. Said detective followed the distraught old man everywhere he went, and everywhere the old man went, the detective found the doctor. The son became tired of waiting for his father's return. The detective informed the son that the father was playing on the emotions of another disturbed individual, a young lady, who fancied herself in love with the doctor. So, the son decided to take it upon himself to warn said doctor. A warning the doctor or his lady friend did not heed, I might add. When the detective followed the old man to a location and saw the young woman throw a bottle at the couple he was to protect and then learned that in the confusion, the old man had gotten away and committed arson, the son decided to intervene. When he did, he took the old man and the girl home. The detective, on a wild hunch, decided to wait around and keep an eye on the doctor. Do I need to say more?"

Micah lowered the gun. "No, sir. So, all the times that I saw you, you'd been following Bates to protect me."

Ford nodded. "You got it. I don't believe that in all

my years in law enforcement I've ever ended up in a mess."

"What are we going to do with him?" Micah pointed to Bates.

"Micah, I think we should let him go home to his son. He needs help," Madison said.

"He needs commitment," Ford interjected. "Not incarceration. I'm sure you can understand."

Micah nodded. "You'll see he gets home to Liam?"

"And I'll make sure he stays there. I have no intention of coming back here again." The man's serious face lightened as he smiled. "I'm glad you understand."

"Yeah, well, I do. All except one thing."

"What's that?" He prodded Bates to walk along while he held a tight grip on his arm.

"Why'd you take so long to call out from above?"

Ford furrowed his brows. "I didn't call out. I wanted the element of surprise."

"No," Micah shook his head adamantly. "You heard him, right, Madison?"

"You called Mr. Bates name," she concurred.

"No, ma'am. I surely did not."

Bates looked up at them with eyes nearly closed shut. "It was God."

Chapter Thirty-One

Madison peeled potatoes and glanced at the calendar in the kitchen. A whole month since the ordeal with Mr. Bates. She peeked in the laundry room where Ashton had gone with a pile of linens. "Another two weeks, and I'll be in school."

Ashton walked out, her eyes wide with mock horror, her hands on the sides of her head. "What am I going to do when you're gone? I simply can't run this inn without you. Are you sure you won't reconsider and stay here permanently?"

Madison chuckled at her friend's melodrama. "You know I'd like to, but I've got juniors and seniors depending on me to help them pass college entrance exams."

"I don't want to, but I guess I'll have to hire someone else." She gave a loud, exaggerated sigh. "How's Micah doing?"

Micah. The sound of his name made her heart pound. "He's met all the requirements to practice in Washington, closed the deal on his medical office, and has begun furnishing the interior. He said he already has people inquiring as to when he'll open his practice."

"Any word on Mr. Bates?"

"Liam, Mr. Bates's son, called Micah to tell him that his father is doing well. He's in a mental facility, and Liam is thankful that we didn't press charges. He's vowed to keep his father committed until they know he isn't a danger any longer, and he'll make us aware of his release."

"That's good."

"And he's dating Victoria." Madison shivered. "He knows about her uncontrolled temper, and he says they're going to counseling together."

"Wow!" Ashton stepped closer. "Love sure comes at us in different ways, doesn't it? I keep waiting to see a ring on that finger."

"Any day now. I hope." Madison attempted to put a bright smile in place, but if truth were told, she'd expected a proposal before now."

Ashton hugged Madison's shoulders. "Honey, I know that look. You're disappointed. Don't worry. It'll happen soon. I need to get back to the wash. Love ya."

"Love you, too, my friend." She put the potatoes on to boil for potato salad and then remembered the call she wanted to make. She pulled her cell from her pocket and walked onto the deck. After punching the number, her stomach whirled. Yes, she was doing the right thing.

"Hello, Madison? I'm surprised to hear from you." Josh's familiar voice used to make her heart pound but no more.

"Hey, Josh. Got a minute?"

"Of course. I'm in Colorado. I interviewed for a job and got hired."

"Oh, I'm glad. What kind of job?"

"Promise not to laugh?"

"Er, uh, yes." She couldn't imagine what type of work he would do besides teaching.

"Remember how I always loved to go fishing?"

"Yeah. You'd take off after school most days in the spring to go to the stream."

"I decided life was too short not to do something I enjoy."

"I thought you loved teaching."

"I do, and I'll get back to it one of these days. But for now, I'm going to be a fishing guide in the trout waters of the Upper Colorado River."

Madison couldn't help but giggle. Josh. Good old unpredictable Josh. "I called for a reason. I need to tell you I believe you now. That you were telling me the truth and wanted to apologize. I'm sorry for not trusting you."

"I'm glad you found it in your heart to forgive me. I see now how wrong I was."

"What's made the change?"

"I don't know. Maybe I've finally become an adult."

"That's wonderful, Josh. And I wish you the best on the wild rapids of Colorado." Madison took a deep breath. To be free of the burden of unforgiveness and doubt toward Josh lifted the weight she hadn't realized she'd carried. Now if only she knew whether Micah wanted to make a life with her. Sometimes, she couldn't help but doubt that he did.

Micah peeked into his future examination room with the cabinet equipped with adhesive bandages, a blood pressure cuff, gloves, and his stethoscopes. The exam table sat against the opposite wall. His pressure pounded harder when he realized he'd open soon. Dr. Micah Collins, MD would soon receive patients. He only had to hire a nurse and a receptionist. For the last month, he'd thought of nothing else besides opening his practice.

Micah walked into the newly redecorated waiting room and admired the freshly painted wall, the contemporary décor, and new wood floors. Though he had enough in savings to get started, a business loan sounded more expedient. Hopefully, he'd have the balance paid off soon.

Madison's beautiful face crept into his mind sending sparks like the fourth of July into his heart. He didn't want to wait another day to ask her to marry him. But how? He had to create a memorable moment.

Micah closed and locked his office door. In his car, he picked up a brochure lying on the front passenger seat. Things to do and see in Cranberry Cove. He flipped through and stopped when he came to the page which featured the city park. The spot where Madison prayed to ask Jesus into her heart. Maybe that would make a good place to propose.

An idea he'd seen once on TV popped into his mind. A guy created a treasure hunt for his fiancé-to-be. That was it. He could do something similar with a few modifications so he wouldn't send Madison all over town.

He pulled into his apartment and rushed in the front door. Inside, he opened the top drawer on his cabinet and found three by five cards. Thinking about their relationship, he could name a dozen times when she'd thought only of him.

He laughed and sat down to write the cards. On the

first, he copied from Mark 10: "Whoever wants to become great among you will be your servant." Madison, you gave me a ride when I had a flat tire.

On the second card, he copied part of Galatians 5:13. "Serve one another with love." Madison, you served me and the people of Cranberry Cove through your help in setting up the caring center.

One more. On the third card, he copied a portion of 1Peter 4:10. "Just as each one has received a gift, use it to serve others." Madison, you gave your spare time to Ashton this summer to help her at the inn.

Micah stood and stretched his arms a moment. He'd do one more, and then on the fifth note, he'd ask her to marry him. He pumped his fist in the air. Perfect. She'd love this proposal. Afterward they could toast their engagement with a bottle of sparkling cider.

On the fourth card, he copied 1John 3:18. "Little children, let us not love in word or speech, but in action and in truth." Madison, you accompanied me to my real-estate dealings and helped me make wise decisions.

Finally, on the fifth card he wrote. Will you bless me by becoming my wife? Even as he wrote the words, his heart beat faster. He prayed Madison would be his for as long as they both lived.

Then another idea impacted his brain. First, he'd head to Oceanview and the Hobby House. He could accomplish both tasks when he made a trip to the jewelry store. Then he'd ask Blake to watch over the notes until he and Madison arrived and to take pictures without her seeing him.

"Wear hiking shoes. We're going on another excursion," Micah had said when he phoned her last night.

In her apartment, Madison glanced at herself in the mirror. Matching leggings and sleeveless knit shirt would work on the trails.

Hiking with Micah. Her pulse raced. For the last month, he'd been so occupied with getting his office ready, they hadn't gone anywhere. She'd helped him some, but setting up her classroom and working for Ashton at the inn had occupied most of her time.

A knock at her door told her Micah had arrived. He walked in, and then he stared at her, mouth hanging open. "You look, er, great. I mean those hiking clothes fit you—er, never mind."

Madison grinned. "Should I change?"

He gave a few vigorous shakes of his head. "No. I mean, I think you'll be fine."

She'd never seen Micah at a loss of words. She grabbed her backpack and retied her shoes. "So, we're not going to the lavender farm this time?"

"Nope."

"Do I need a blindfold again?"

"Not this time."

Twenty minutes later, Micah pulled into the city park. Again, she'd never seen him so nervous. Maybe he'd had a hard week or made a lot of difficult decisions. He slipped a backpack on his back and reached for her hand.

They hiked down the same trail to the picnic tables about a mile away. Micah sat her down at the table to her right. "The Sunday you asked the Lord in your life, we came here."

She smiled. "I remember."

"Today there are a series of papers attached to the trees and bushes by a red ribbon."

"What?" Madison smiled and glanced at a tree branch. She spotted a card attached to a red bow. Then a length of ribbon extended from the tree to a bush about twenty feet away.

"After you read the first note, follow the ribbon to help you find the next."

For a moment, Madison had hoped Micah would propose, but he only need one note for that. Her longing would have to wait until another day. But nevertheless, she'd play along.

She read the first card and smiled. "I was happy to give you a ride. Besides, I couldn't wait to get to know the handsome doctor I'd just met."

Micah kissed her on the nose and laughed. "Follow the ribbon."

Madison trekked along the trail, the red ribbon showing her the way.

A thud and a rustling of bushes to her right caused her to yelp. "Micah, I think there're bears out here."

Micah, who'd followed behind her, threw his arms around her. "You're safe with me. I'll protect you if one happens to make an appearance." With the wide grin and laughter in his eyes, Micah no doubt didn't fear a wild animal. He glanced toward the bushes, shook his head, and frowned.

Micah was signaling bears? Crazy.

She continued the hunt for notes until she finally came to number four. She read it and smiled. "I loved helping with your real-estate choices."

Micah danced around from one foot to the other. "Okay, now for number five."

She followed the ribbon which wound around a couple of bushes. About forty feet off the trail, she picked up the last one and read. Tears formed in her eyes as she repeated the message. "Will you bless me by becoming my wife?" she whispered.

In front of her, Micah bent on one knee. He held up a gorgeous marquise diamond ring in a purple velvet box. "Madison Mitchell. I've loved you from the day you found the Savior. You are truly a servant of God. Will you marry me?"

Madison grasped her neck and breathed deeply. "I think I've loved you since the day you forgave me for knocking you in the head with a fishing rod."

Micah, still on his knees, laughed.

"Or maybe it was when we encountered Ford with his binoculars. You always nudged me behind you, ready to protect me from danger." She leaned down to give him a kiss on his cheek. "Yes, Dr. Micah Collins, I'd love to marry you."

Micah bound to his feet and slipped the diamond on her finger. "Yahoo," he yelled. He drew her into his arms, and his warm lips covered hers. When he finally released her, he murmured. "That outfit you're wearing makes me wish the wedding was tonight." He nuzzled her chin.

The bushes rustled once more. "Can you do the kiss again? I didn't get a good shot."

Madison jumped and wrapped her arms around Micah. "Who…?" She looked at the person who'd spoken. "Blake Sloan." Her mouth fell open.

"I'm sorry about the noise a while ago. I stumbled

over some root, but don't worry, I got some great shots as well as video footage." He laughed. "All except that kiss."

Micah wrapped his arms around Madison again. "I'm sorry, but I have to kiss you again."

She only knew Micah's arms around her and his lips on hers. Imagine, the man kissing her was to be her husband soon. She ran her fingers along Micah's neck and determined to ignore Blake while he took the pictures.

226

Chapter Thirty-Two

One month later

Madison twirled around before the floor-length mirror in the inn's newly converted bridal suite. Her form-fitting bridal gown flared at her knees. She fingered the lacy sleeveless bodice with the jeweled neckline. "I love your new accommodations for brides."

Her maid-of-honor adjusted the straps of her soft floral gown. "One day we'd like to build another wing. We're expanding our facilities to a wedding venue."

"You and James will make a success of your new venture."

Ashton giggled and picked up the picture album of Micah's proposal. "Blake's a good photographer. I laugh every time I remember your story of how you thought you'd encountered a bear. I can't wait to see the video."

Madison laughed. "The rustling in the bushes—I couldn't help but think some sort of animal was after us."

Ashton opened to the last page. "This is my favorite."

An unusual flush warmed Madison's face. "We didn't allow a photographer to distract us."

"Such a dreamy kiss." Ashton sighed. "I'm a hopeless

romantic."

A soft tap on the door sent Ashton to answer. "Gracie. How's the new mama?"

"Blake and I are in love with our daughter. I have someone who'd like to speak to Madison."

Ashton turned to Madison, a question on her face.

Madison glanced at the woman with Gracie. "Victoria, you and Gracie please come in."

Victoria approached, her steps slow and hesitant. "I wanted to congratulate you on your wedding—and show you my ring." She held out her left ring finger.

Madison took her hand and gazed at the beautiful diamond Victoria wore. "It's beautiful."

"Liam and I are planning a summer wedding." Victoria smiled. "But today, I wanted to thank you for inviting us to your wedding. We hadn't anticipated that you would under the circumstances."

Madison hugged Victoria and stepped back again. "Don't worry about the past. I've made so many mistakes, I couldn't count them all, but God has forgiven me through His Son Jesus."

Victoria winked. "Lately, Liam and I have attended church in Sacramento. Our lives are progressing in a different direction these days."

"I'm so happy for you." Madison fiddled with the silk ribbon around her waist. What about Mr. Bates?"

"He's in a psychiatric hospital on the coast. He was diagnosed with PTED, and he's responding to treatment. Liam and I are in Christian counseling, and I'm learning to deal with my uncontrolled anger impulse. Madison, I did throw that bottle, and I'm grateful that you didn't get serious hurt." Victoria clasped her hands in front of her.

"That's over and done with," Madison assured.

"Thank you, and I'm grateful to help you celebrate this amazing event today. Your marriage to Dr. Micah Collins." Victoria's smile spread across her face.

Another tap sent Ashton to answer the door again. She smiled at the wedding planner from Oceanview.

"The groom and best man are waiting at the altar."

Madison hugged Gracie, and then Victoria and finally Ashton. "I'm ready."

Micah stood tall in his all-white suit, Blake by his side in a green coat and pants. Madison had described his suit as a pale lime ensemble. *Your white and Blake's light green will complement the colors of our garden wedding.*

He didn't care what color his suit was or where they wed. He couldn't wait for Madison to be his.

After Blake left to escort the maid-of-honor, Pastor Ethridge stood on his other side under the flower-covered archway in the rose garden behind the inn.

Micah glanced out at the guests in chairs with blue and pink ribbons on each.

When the string quartet began to play *Pachelbel's Canon in D*, Micah could only think of one thing. Soon the loveliest woman in the world would walk along the path between the rows of chairs. Her mother, whom he'd only met two days ago, agreed to accompany her.

Ashton and Blake arrived, and then he caught his breath.

Madison floated near to face him. Her sweet smile and bright blue eyes sent his pulse racing.

Micah had no trouble repeating vows he intended to

keep as long as he lived.

When her soft voice spoke her vows to love him for as many days God gave them on the earth, she didn't take her eyes off him.

Pastor Ethridge said, "In Genesis, the Bible tells us that a man should leave his father and mother and be joined to his wife, and they will become one flesh. So, by the authority vested in me by the state of Washington, I pronounce you husband and wife. You may now kiss your bride."

Micah took his wife in his arms and kissed her for the first time as Mrs. Madison Collins.

Some ooo's and awh's echoed from the guests who'd gathered to witness their union.

"Allow me to be the first to introduce Dr. and Mrs. Micah Collins." Pastor's voice echoed in his ear as he grasped her hand.

With a wide smile, Micah with Madison by his side, strolled down the aisle. In the large living room, he turned to his bride again and whispered. "Our hotel in Seattle which overlooks Lake Washington is reserved. I can't wait until tonight."

Madison grinned. "I'm glad my principal was so lenient in allowing me time off from school. Two weeks in Bora Bora is the dreamiest location for a honeymoon, I've read."

Micah nuzzled her ear and whispered, "And the most romantic, I've heard."

Madison slipped her arms around him and sighed. "I can never thank you enough for showing me the way to the Savior and a better way of life."

"And I can never thank you for promising to stand by my side as long as we both live."

His lips were still on hers when he heard the sounds of children, the conversations of the adults, and the shuffling of footsteps arriving from the garden. "Until tonight."

Epilogue – one year later

Madison rose from the stool in her art studio at the wharf. A property facing the bay had come on the market, and Micah had encouraged her to take it. Besides, her shop was only a few miles from their new home up the coast.

The two door panels Dr. Greenwood from Oceanview had commissioned her to make for his residence were finally finished. The floor to ceiling shell pattern in grays and silver complimented his décor beautifully, if she did say so herself. The project was her highest sale so far.

She smiled when she felt the flutter in her belly. Her doctor had mentioned she'd feel the baby moving any day now. She rubbed her abdomen and sighed. Speaking of her doctor, she'd better stop by his office and give him a kiss. She grabbed her potato salad from the studio refrigerator and headed for her car.

The last patient walked out of Micah's clinic, a smile on her face. The expectant mother was overjoyed when he'd confirmed her suspicions. He hadn't planned on accepting so many maternity patients, but somehow his case load worked out like that. He grinned. Maternity patients including his wife.

With his nurse and receptionist gone home, he turned

out the lights in back. Before he had a chance to lock the front, the door dinged as someone entered. He headed down the hall and stopped. The most beautiful woman in the world. And now she was giving him a child.

"I need a kiss from my doctor." She threw her arms around him and pressed her lips on his.

After a few moments, he brushed his lips across her chin. "Seriously, don't you think you want to see a gynecologist in Oceanview? A physician treating his own family isn't the norm." He wrapped his arms around her expanding belly and kissed her, not allowing her to answer.

After he pulled away, Madison gazed at him. "Why do I need to go to Oceanview? I have my own gynecologist here in Cranberry Cove. Besides, if I have a homebirth, I don't think it will matter."

He swatted her on the rear. "The sign on the door says I practice internal medicine."

She laughed. "You're responsible for my condition, so the least you can do is be my doctor."

"I love you, Madison, and can't wait to parent our child. If he's a boy, I'll teach him to fish and hike in the woods and— "

"What if she's a girl?"

"Then I'll teach her to how to ride a bike, and take her to a favorite restaurant for father-daughter night."

Madison glanced at her watch. "Sounds wonderful, but right now we need to get to The Caring Center. We're having the potluck tonight, don't forget. I dropped my potato salad off a few minutes ago."

"I might have forgotten if you hadn't mentioned it." He slipped his arm around her shoulders as they walked out the front door and headed up the sidewalk to The

Caring Center. Folks had already started to gather, including Karina, her hair in a short style a lot of the ladies wore. She'd dropped in the office last week to say her doctor pronounced her in a state of remission. Karina had even agreed to lead one of the support groups.

Micah held the door for his wife and caught his breath once again as the truth dawned. Madison was his. He whispered, "Lord, You have blessed me with a wife, a new practice, an amazing home on the bay, and now a child. I will forever exalt You and praise Your name. Amen.

The End

If you enjoyed *A Home in Cranberry Cove*, please consider leaving a review on Amazon.

Sign up for June's newsletter to get the latest about her books

June's Blog - Scroll to the bottom of the page!

In case you missed book one: *The Inn at Cranberry Cove* **– first place 2021 Selah winner in romantic suspense—Blue Ridge Mountain Christian Conference**

Ashton Price arrives in Cranberry Cove, Washington, her pride wounded by her former boss. James Atwood endures punishing guilt after the death of his wife and son. Together, they must discover the mystery that haunts the Inn at Cranberry Cove. Amazon

Book two continues the story: *Love Found at Cranberry Cove*

Gracie Mayberry wants to study marine science at

the community college in a neighboring coastal town. Seattle resident Blake Sloan admits he's followed his father's dream instead of his heart's desire—to run his own business and start a non-profit to benefit wounded vets. But when a stalker makes terrifying midnight visits to the humble Mayberry home and threatens their lives, Blake discovers he's also a target of extortion. Can Blake and Gracie learn who's behind the danger that threatens them? Will a small-town girl and big-city boy find a life together? Amazon

In Book three, visit Cranberry Cove at Christmas: *Christmas at Cranberry Cove*

Ryder Langston retires from commercial fishing and manages Blake Sloan's supply stores. When the owner of the inn in Cranberry Cove hires a new executive chef, Ryder is intrigued by the tall woman with ebony hair who hides a dark family secret.

Juliette Duplay must flee from her French roots and her past when a family member turns against her. She'd like to blend into the American culture but can't escape danger even in the small community of Cranberry Cove.

Can Ryder and Juliette unravel the mystery in time to celebrate *Christmas at Cranberry Cove?*

Also, by June Foster the Almond Tree Series

For All Eternity **book one**

Joella Crawford never expects to meet the man of her dreams when she plows over handsome JD Neilson with her bicycle on a beautiful summer day in northern California. She can't leave the gorgeous guy lying on the ground with a bloody leg so she administers first aid. Now she's convinced she's met the man of her dreams. He's a successful young accountant with impeccable manners. When JD walks out of her life, she turns to her friend David Reyes. But she can't deny her feelings for JD.

JD Neilson has to admit he's hopelessly in love with classy interior designer, Joella Crawford, despite his father's objections. After threats to disown him, JD finally succumbs to his dad's demands and dates a woman who is more acceptable in his family's opinion. But on the eve of his wedding to the other woman, he can't forget the woman he adores—and his reasons for loving her. Will he marry the wrong person, or will he follow his heart? Amazon

Echoes from the Past **book two**

When Dave Reyes, senior pastor of New Life Fellowship discovers he has a six-year-old daughter, his life changes forever. He must reveal the truth to the congregation, but will they fire him and send him away in shame?

Social worker Betty Ann Johnston still grieves over the death of her police officer husband. But when he returns from the grave to torment her, she struggles to maintain her sanity. Witnessing Dave's faith is her only source of strength. Will ghosts from her past destroy her, or will she find hope in the God of the Bible?

Amazon

What God Knew **book three**
Tammy Crawford wants nothing to do with her sister Joella's religion but when she falls in love with handsome Dr. Michael Clark, he challenges her long-held resistance. Can two people of different races and beliefs find a life together? Amazon

Almond Street Mission **book four**
When Glorilyn Neilson's nineteen-year-old brother, Tannon, goes missing without a trace, she's frantic. Prayer and volunteering at the local homeless shelter in El Camino must fill the time until her sibling returns. But her sapphire eyes and auburn hair inadvertently cause a stir among the male population at the center. Her life changes one evening when she's attacked by a burly vagrant intent on rape in the alley behind the building.

Jeremiah Goodman loves the Lord, but he's homeless. When he witnesses a foul-mouthed vagrant overpowering one of the volunteers at the homeless shelter, he defends her, saving her from unwanted advances.

When Glorilyn offers Jeremiah a way of escape from his impoverished lifestyle, he can't tell her why he must live the life of a vagrant. What powerful secret keeps him on the streets? Amazon

About June Foster
An award-winning and bestselling author, June Foster is also a retired teacher with a BA in Education and a MA in counseling. She is the mother of two and grandmother of ten. June began writing Christian romance in 2010. She penned her first novel on her Toshiba laptop as she and her husband traveled the US in their RV. Her adventures provide a rich source of information for her novels. She brags about visiting a location before it becomes the setting in her next book.

To date, June has written thirty contemporary romance and romantic suspense novels and novellas. She loves to compose stories about characters who overcome the circumstances in their lives by the power of God and His Word. June uses her training in counseling and her Christian beliefs in creating characters who find freedom to live godly lives. She's published with Winged Publications. Visit June at June's books to see a complete list of her books.

Find June at:

Amazon Author Page
Twitter
Facebook
June's website

Enjoy these books by June Foster
The Woodlyn Series
Flawless
Out of Control
All Things New

The Almond Tree Series
For All Eternity
Echoes From the Past
What God Knew
Almond Street Mission

Small Town Romance
Letting Go
Prescription for Romance
A Harvest of Blessings
The Long Way Home

The Cranberry Cove Series
The Inn at Cranberry Cove
Love Found at Cranberry Cove
Christmas at Cranberry Cove

Christmas Novellas
Christmas at Raccoon Creek
A Christmas Kiss
A Kiss Under the Mistletoe

Devotional
Dancing in a Field of Daisies

Short Stories
Someone to Call His Own
An Accidental Kiss

Stand Alone Titles
Red and the Wolf